❦ BOOK REVIEWS

Here's what people are saying:

A lighthearted, humorous look at the nature of responsibility, with all three boys distinct individuals.

from KIRKUS

A sensitive subject handled realistically and convincingly.

from BOOKLIST

This has guaranteed appeal for middle-grade boys.

from BULLETIN OF THE CENTER FOR CHILDRENS BOOKS

JUST FOR BOYS® PRESENTS

Kidnapping Kevin Kowalski

MARY JANE AUCH

HOLIDAY HOUSE/NEW YORK

For Nancy Buss, Mary C. Ryan, and Margery Facklam—
the best critics and friends a writer ever had

————————

Special thanks to Jerid M. Fisher, Ph.D.,
Neurorehab Associates, Rochester, New York,
for his technical help

Copyright © 1990 by Mary Jane Auch
All rights reserved
Printed in the United States of America
First Edition
Library of Congress Cataloging-in-Publication Data

Auch, Mary Jane.
Kidnapping Kevin Kowalski / by Mary Jane Auch.—1st ed.
p. cm.
Summary: When a terrible accident partially disables Kevin and
makes his mother overprotective of him, his best friends Ryan and
Mooch decide that the only way to liberate him is to kidnap him.
ISBN 0-8234-0815-9
[1. Friendship—Fiction. 2. Mothers and sons—Fiction.
3. Kidnapping—Fiction.] I. Title.
PZ7.A898Ki 1990
[Fic]—dc20 89-46065 CIP AC

Kidnapping Kevin Kowalski

Chapter 1

"What do you think Kevin's going to look like, Ryan?" Mooch asked.

"Why should he look any different?" I said.

"He's been in the hospital a long time. Who knows what they did to him?"

"He must be okay now, or they wouldn't have let him come home. Besides, he was only in the hospital for the first couple of weeks. Then he was in a rehab center out in Chicago."

Mooch shrugged. "Same thing."

"It is not. A rehab center isn't for real sick people, like a hospital. My dad told me they do exercises and stuff. Kev is probably in great shape by now."

"Yeah, maybe." Mooch ran a couple of steps to catch up, since his legs were so much shorter than mine. "But my brother says he's probably got a steel plate in his head. You think we'll be able to see the screws through his skin?"

Mooch always asked a lot of stupid questions. I tried to ignore him, but he kept right on running off at the mouth. "He's supposed to have brain damage from hitting the pavement. You think that means he's going to be a dummy?"

I gave him a shove. "No dumber than you."

Mooch scrambled to get his balance and pulled his T-shirt down over his fat stomach. "No kidding, Ryan. I don't think they'll let him come back to school with us. He already missed the whole last month of sixth grade, and you get more work than ever in seventh. How's he going to do it, if he's . . ."

"If he's what?" I snarled.

"If he's, you know, not right in the head," Mooch said. "We haven't even seen him for over two whole months, Ryan. Who knows what he's like?"

"If you're going to go over to Kevin's house and act like he's some sort of freak, you can get lost right now."

"He's my friend as much as yours." Mooch was trotting now, trying to keep up. "Just because you were the one riding bikes with him when he got hit, that doesn't put you in charge."

"Knock it off. Here's his house. You want him to hear you?"

Mooch shoved in close to me as we started up the Kowalskis' front walk. "I just think we oughta be ready for him to be different, that's all."

I jutted out my chin and rang the doorbell. "I'm ready," I said, only I knew I wasn't. I'd known Kevin and Mooch ever since kindergarten. Kevin had always been the leader, the one to come up with wild schemes. When he'd been away for the past two months, Mooch and I had sat around, saying, "I don't know. What do *you* want to do?" What if Mooch was right? What if Kevin was different now?

I didn't have much time to worry about it, because Mrs. Kowalski opened the door. "Oh, hi, kids. I didn't expect Kevin to have visitors so soon after he got home." She ran her fingers through her short red hair. When she smiled she looked a lot like Kevin, but she wasn't smiling now.

Suddenly I was afraid to see Kevin. What if he was completely changed? Weird, even. "Maybe we should've called first," I said. "We can come back another time, Mrs. Kowalski."

"Yes, well . . ." Mrs. Kowalski looked over her shoulder. "As long as you're here, you might as well go in."

"No really," I said, backing off. "If this isn't a good time . . ."

It was too late. Mooch was already through the door.

"You'll have to make this a short visit," Mrs. Kowalski said, "because Kevin tends to tire easily."

She led us into the living room where the TV was

blasting. At first, all we could see was the back of Kevin's head. It was covered with his red curly hair, so you couldn't see any screws.

Kevin never heard us until we got right in front of him. He was sitting on the couch, staring at the set with his mouth sort of hanging open.

"Look who came to visit you, Kevin," Mrs. Kowalski said.

Kevin's eyes brightened as soon as he saw us. "Ryan, Mooch! I sure have missed you guys."

Mrs. Kowalski fluffed the pillow behind Kevin's back. "Don't tire yourself out now, dear. I'll go and get some snacks for you and the boys."

I sat down next to Kevin on the couch, and Mooch plopped into the chair across from us. "How are you doing?" I asked. Kevin held his left arm down close to his side. I could tell there was something funny about that arm, but I looked him in the eye, so he wouldn't think I was staring.

"I'm okay, I guess," Kevin said.

"You could have called, you know," Mooch said. "How were we supposed to know you got home three days ago?"

A strange look passed over Kevin's face. "Well, I was going to call. I just didn't get a chance. I've been really busy since I got back."

"Doing what?" Mooch asked.

Kevin shrugged. "Just . . . things." He looked

different somehow. For one thing, I wasn't used to him just sitting, not doing anything. Before the accident, he was constantly moving—tapping his foot on the floor or drumming his fingers on the table. He even thrashed around the bed when he was asleep. He looked pale now, too. By this time of year he usually had a whole mess of freckles from being out in the sun. And there was a look in his eyes that was different.

"So, where's the plate?" Mooch asked, breaking the silence. I couldn't kick him because he was too far away.

"You mean the snacks?" Kevin asked. "Give my mother a break, will you? She only left the room a few minutes ago. You want fast food, go to McDonald's."

"No, the *steel* plate," Mooch said, "the one in your head."

If *I*'d had a steel plate, I would've slipped it into Mooch's head right then and there We had planned to let Kevin bring up the accident, but Mooch had to start asking questions.

Kevin didn't seem to mind, though. "There's no steel plate. Just a scar where they operated." He leaned forward and parted his hair with his fingers. "See?"

I didn't want to see it, but Mooch leaned closer for a better look. He let out a low whistle. "Neat-o!

Look at this, Ryan. They sewed right up the side of Kev's head. They got a machine that does that?"

My stomach did a slow flip.

Kevin laughed. "Sure. They stick your head in this big sewing machine and zip it right up." He shook his head. "Boy, I sure have missed all your dumb questions, Mooch. So what went on in school while I was away?"

"Nothing much," Mooch said. "We didn't do anything. They even canceled the fossil-hunt field trip because of the weather. Too bad you weren't there for sixth-grade graduation, though. Cindy Gunther wore a strapless dress. You shoulda seen it."

"Really?" Kevin asked, grinning. "Cindy sure must have changed a lot in the past two months. Last time I saw her, she couldn't have held up a strapless dress."

"It was probably padding, don't you think, Ryan?" Mooch asked.

"I don't know. I didn't notice."

Mooch stretched out and put his feet on the coffee table. "Ryan didn't have time to notice because he was too busy running up to get all his awards. He got almost all of the dumb academic stuff—math, science, social studies, even the good citizenship award, better known as the teacher's pet award."

"Mooch got an award, too," I said. "He was voted 'most likely not to care if he doesn't succeed.' "

Mooch ignored my remark. "Everybody was asking about you, Kev, wondering when you'd get back."

"Yeah," I added, "the sixth grade chorus sang 'You'll Never Walk Alone' and dedicated it to you."

"Thanks a bunch," Kevin said. "Did they think I was going to end up a cripple or something?"

I could feel my face getting red. "I never thought of it that way. I know that's not how they meant it."

Mooch looked puzzled. "Oh, I get it," he said finally, slapping his knee. "You mean you'll never walk alone, like you'll have to have somebody hold you up or be in a wheelchair or something. That's a good one, Kevin. We'll have to remember that one to tell at scout camp."

I shot Mooch a look. The other thing we agreed not to mention was camp, at least not until we knew whether Kevin would be able to go or not.

"I'd forgotten all about camp," Kevin said. "When are we supposed to sign up?"

"We did it last month," Mooch said.

"You put my name in, didn't you?"

I looked away. "We weren't sure if you'd still want to go."

"What are you, kidding? Why wouldn't I want to go? Have I ever missed a year of scout camp?"

I fussed with the doily on the arm of the couch,

smoothing out the wrinkles. "We just didn't know . . ."

"Didn't know what?"

"Oh, come off it," Mooch said. "I'll say it, if Ryan won't. For all we knew, you'd come back as a vegetable. How did we know what you'd be like after your brains got spilled all over Ridge Road?"

"Shut up, Mooch," I said. "Do you always have to say the first dumb thing that comes into your head?"

"Is that what you guys thought," Kevin asked, looking at me, "that I'd be some sort of a freak?"

Mooch took his feet off the table and leaned forward. "Yeah. *Are* you?"

"I told you before, I'm okay. And thanks a bunch for leaving me out of the plans for camp. I'm still going."

Mrs. Kowalski came in and set a big bowl of popcorn on the coffee table. "Going where, dear?"

"Scout camp is next month, Mom," Kevin said.

"Oh?" From the look on her face, I had the feeling Mrs. Kowalski wasn't wild about Kevin heading off to the Adirondacks with a backpack.

"We can all ride up together," I offered. "My folks just got that van we were talking about, so there's plenty of room for all of us and our junk."

Mrs. Kowalski cleared her throat. "That's very nice of you and your parents, Ryan, but I don't think Kevin will be needing a ride to camp."

"But I can go, can't I, Mom?"

"We'll see, dear."

"He's got to go, Mrs. Kowalski," Mooch said. "We're going to Massaweepie this year. It's the best scout camp around. They've got everything— swimming, boating, even rappeling."

"Yes . . . well, we'll see," Mrs. Kowalski said as she left the room.

Mooch frowned. "When my mom says that, she means no."

"Since when has your mother ever cared what you do?" Kevin said, slumping down into the couch. "You're right, though. She'll never let me go."

"You gotta," Mooch said. "My cousin Frankie's troop went to Massawepie right after school let out. He said they have this great-looking girl for a waterfront counselor."

"A girl counselor in a Boy Scout camp?" I asked. "Your cousin needs glasses."

"No, honest, Frankie practically fell in love with her. He never swam a stroke in his life before this summer, and he came home from camp with his lifesaving badge. I think he only got out of the water to eat." Mooch grabbed two fistfuls of popcorn and spilled half of it on the rug.

"You have the eating habits of a warthog," I said. "You'd better pick that up before Kevin's mother comes back."

"No sweat," Kevin said, spilling a few kernels of popcorn himself. "She doesn't yell at me anymore. I bet I could do almost anything and she wouldn't say a word."

"That must be great," Mooch said. "The only time my ma ever talks to me is when she's yelling at me for something. Maybe I oughta go get my head bashed in so she'll start treating me decent. Then I could go to one of those fancy rehash centers and build up my muscles." He dropped to his knees and set his elbow on the coffee table. "Hey, Kev, you wanna see if you can beat me at arm wrestling, now that you've been working out?"

"He could beat you at arm wrestling *before* he was working out," I said.

"Yeah," Kevin said. "Besides, I don't feel like arm wrestling."

"What's the matter, Kev?" Mooch tucked his hands in his armpits and flapped his elbows like chicken wings, making clucking noises. "Are you too chicken?"

"You asked for it," Kevin said, getting down on his knees across from Mooch. He planted his right elbow firmly on the table and grabbed Mooch's hand.

"You sure you're supposed to be doing this?" I asked.

Kevin looked at me. "You sound like my mother. Give us a starting signal, will you?"

When I gave the signal, they both started pushing. It looked pretty even at first, then I noticed something strange about Kevin. He was wrestling with his right hand, but his left arm started to tighten up, and his fingers gradually curled into a tight fist. He was getting real red in the face, when all of a sudden he just gave up. Mooch pushed his arm back on the table with a thud, and the bowl of popcorn spilled all over the rug.

Mrs. Kowalski came into the room so fast, I thought she had radar. "What's going on here? Malcolm, what are you doing to poor Kevin?"

Nobody but Mrs. Kowalski ever called Mooch by his real name. "I'm sorry, Mrs. Kowalski. We were just fooling around. Right, Kev?"

"Relax, Mom," Kevin said, "I'm fine." He tried to pull himself back up onto the couch, but his left leg buckled under him.

Mrs. Kowalski put her hands under his arms and hauled him up. "Don't you know that fooling around could put you right back into the hospital?" She settled him on the couch, brushing the hair back from his eyes. "You're not even wearing your helmet." She turned and glared at me. "You ought to know it was fooling around that made Kevin into . . . that caused his problem in the first place."

What was she talking about? Kevin's getting hit was an accident, and it didn't have anything to do with me. I was just there. And what was she going to say? Made Kevin into a what?

Kevin's left arm was pulled up tight now. He rubbed the fingers of his left hand, trying to straighten them out on the arm of the couch. "Don't yell at the guys, Mom. We were just having fun."

Kevin's mother went over to the front door and opened it. "I think you and the guys have had enough fun for one day."

Mooch was still on the floor, inhaling popcorn like a human vacuum cleaner. I nudged him with my foot. "Come on, Mooch, I gotta get home."

As we went out the door, Mrs. Kowalski said, "Next time, I'd appreciate it if you'd call first."

I looked back over my shoulder. Kevin was staring at the TV again, as if we'd never been there at all.

Chapter 2

I walked so fast, Mooch couldn't catch up with me all the way back to my house. When I stormed into the kitchen, Dad was stirring spaghetti sauce and Mom was clearing the kitchen table, shoving everything to one end. She picked up some junk mail that had slipped off the edge of the table onto the floor. "Oh good, you're home. I was just about to call Mooch's house to see if you were there."

Mooch was right behind me. "Boy, that sure smells good. Spaghetti is just about my favorite thing in the whole world, you know."

Dad grinned. "We know, Mooch. You've managed to fit that into the conversation at least once a week, usually on the night we're having spaghetti."

Mooch moved toward the cupboard. "You want me to help set the table, Mrs. Zeigler? I know where everything is."

"Sure, Mooch, I never turn down an offer of help." Mom gave me a meaningful look.

Mooch grabbed five plates from the cupboard and started setting the table.

Mom smiled. "Since you seem to have an extra plate there by mistake, maybe you'd like to stay for dinner."

Mooch tried to look surprised at the number of plates he'd set out. "How did I do that? Well, sure, if it's no trouble. I'll call my mother, so she doesn't worry about me being late getting home."

That was how Mooch got his nickname. He could mooch anything from anybody. The bit about calling his mother was a con, too. Mrs. Manuse wouldn't worry about Mooch if he were hitchhiking to Alaska. She had raised seven kids by herself, and Mooch and his big brother Gary were the only ones left at home. As far as I could see, Mrs. Manuse expected them to raise themselves, which probably explained why Mooch ate over at our house so much.

My older sister, Brenda, burst through the kitchen door. She started to dump her beach bag on the kitchen table, but Mom grabbed it in mid-dump and shoved it back at her. "If people would stop using this table as a loading dock, we might be able to eat off it once in a while."

"Sorry, Mom. What's for dinner?"

"Spaghetti," Mooch said, putting out the silverware.

"Did you adopt him when I wasn't looking?" Brenda asked. "That kid gets more meals here than I do."

"He also helps out around here more than you do," Mom said, "so it all evens out."

Brenda curled her lip at Mooch and went to dump her beach stuff in the living room.

"Come and get it," Dad said, draining the spaghetti over the sink. Mooch was the first one in line, and later, the first one back for seconds.

"So, did you get to see Kevin this afternoon?" Mom asked.

"Yeah," I said.

"How's he doing?" Dad asked.

I shrugged. "Okay."

"Come off it, Ryan." Mooch slurped up a piece of spaghetti that dangled off his lower lip. "He isn't all right. He's weird."

Brenda rolled her eyes. "This is news?" Brenda felt she had an automatic right to insult anybody who was a friend of mine.

"I saw Kevin's father at Rotary last week," Dad said. "He told me the doctors at the rehab center said Kevin was coming along well."

"He is," I said. "There's just something about his arm that doesn't look right."

"There's something else about him, too," Mooch said. "He seems different."

"You're crazy," I said, but I knew what Mooch meant.

Mooch wound a wad of spaghetti the size of a baseball around his fork. "Kev's mother knows something's wrong. She's not going to let him go to camp."

"Camp is a whole month away," Mom said. "Kevin could improve a lot by then. I'm sure his mother will change her mind."

Dad broke off a big hunk of garlic bread. "He's going to be having physical therapy three times a week. That should help. Is he walking okay?"

I shrugged. "I don't know. He never stood up."

"Well, I think your mother's right," Dad said. "Give it some time. He's been through a lot."

The next day I went over to see Kevin without Mooch. I called first and got the okay from Mrs. Kowalski. He was watching TV again when I got there.

"No arm wrestling today," Mrs. Kowalski said. "Got that?" She waited until I agreed before she left the room.

"Where's Mooch?" Kevin asked.

"That's a great welcome. I come over to see you and all I get is 'Where's Mooch?' We need to make plans for camp, and I figured it would be easier without Mooch sticking in his two cents every other minute."

"What kind of plans?"

"Well, first of all, you need to get in practice."

"For what?"

"For the stuff we're going to be doing at camp—like hiking, for instance."

"I can't go on any hikes," Kevin said. "Besides, Mom is never going to let me go to camp, so what's the use?"

"Don't worry about that right now. Let's go out for a walk."

Kevin didn't make a move to get up. "Not now. I don't feel like it."

He leaned his head back on the couch pillow and closed his eyes for a few seconds. I didn't want to come right out and ask him, but I hadn't seen him stand up yet. And his mother had had to pull him up onto the couch yesterday. Maybe he was just trying to cover up. Maybe he was afraid to let me know he couldn't walk anymore. Maybe . . .

"What are you staring at?" Kevin asked. "You're acting as if you're in a trance or something."

"Why don't we go up to your room?" I said. "Let's look at your baseball cards."

Kevin glanced over at the stairs. "Nah, I don't feel like it."

"Look," I said, taking the plunge, "I have to know. Can you walk or not?"

"Sure I can walk. I just can't go too far at one time, that's all. I get tired faster than I used to."

"No problem. We'll start with short distances and work up."

Just then we heard a car come into the driveway. "Dad's home," Kevin said, changing the subject.

Mrs. Kowalski looked in on us. "Now that your father's here, I'm going to the store, Kevin. If you need anything, just call for him."

"Okay, Mom."

"Don't they ever leave you alone anymore?" I asked, after she left.

"Sure I can be left alone. She was just waiting for Dad to come home with the car."

"What's wrong with her car?"

"I don't know. Why are you asking so many questions?"

"Sorry."

"Hey, Ryan!" Kevin's dad came in, smiling. "Good to have you hanging around here again. I've missed seeing Kevin's buddies." He sat down next to Kevin and leaned forward, his elbows on his knees.

"Yeah, it's good to see you, too, Mr. Kowalski."

"So what big plans do you have for the summer? Going on any trips this year?"

"Probably not," I said. "Dad took most of his vacation time when we went to Disney World at Easter. I'm going to camp, though."

Mr. Kowalski looked thoughtfully at Kevin. "That's right. Your scout troop usually goes camping in August. We'd better start thinking about what you'll need, Kevin."

Kevin stared at the TV. "Sure, Dad."

"Well, you guys enjoy yourselves. I'm going to go weed the garden."

When Mr. Kowalski left, I said, "They're going to let you go to camp, Kev. Your dad just said so."

"My dad isn't the one who makes the decisions around here. At least not since the accident. He and Mom argue a lot, and he always lets her win."

He looked upset, so it was my turn to change the subject. "It's hot in here. How about going outside for a while?"

I watched as he got up off the couch. I could see that his left leg wasn't working quite right, but he managed. He hung onto the railing going down the back steps, but once he got on level ground, he walked okay.

Kevin's younger sister, Emily, was playing with her cat under a tree. "Hi, pip-squeak," I called, but she wouldn't look up. "What's with her?"

"I don't know. She's turning into a real pain."

"Sisters are like that," I said. "Brenda turned into

a real pain when she was about Emily's age. She's ten, isn't she?"

Kevin shrugged. "Yeah, I guess so."

"Well, get used to it. It only gets worse."

Kevin was edging back toward the house, so I had to think of something to do. "Want to go down to the creek? It should be cooler there. I heard a big bullfrog croaking the other night. Maybe we could find him."

"I don't know if I should." Kevin looked over his shoulder. His father was working in the garden.

"You want me to ask your dad if it's all right?"

"Yeah, I guess." Kevin sat on the steps while I ran back to the garden and asked Mr. Kowalski.

"Sure, Ryan, that's a great idea," Mr. Kowalski said, wiping the sweat off his forehead. "Kevin's supposed to be trying to do a little more each day."

"I promise I won't let him get too tired," I said.

"Don't worry about it. He's been a real lounge lizard lately. The exercise will be good for him."

I tried to walk slowly, so Kevin wouldn't have trouble keeping up, and he seemed to be moving along pretty well. His father waved as we went by the garden.

We sat on a big rock that jutted halfway out into the creek and listened for frogs. Kevin seemed to relax. We'd always spent a lot of time at the creek, and he loved it. After a while, Kevin said, "I don't remember anything about what happened that day."

"What day?" I asked, playing dumb.

"You know. The day of the accident. Did you see me get . . . hit?" He shivered a little.

"Sort of." I tossed a stone into the deepest part of the creek, waiting to hear the thunk as it hit the bottom. I could see the whole thing—Kevin riding no hands ahead of me on his ten-speed. I could see his face as he turned to yell something over his shoulder, and the way his expression changed when he saw the car. I could hear the guy laying on his horn, and I could feel the heat from the engine of his car as it skimmed past me. But I couldn't picture Kevin actually getting hit.

"What do you mean, 'sort of'?" Kevin asked. I felt his eyes on me.

"I don't remember much either. I just saw you . . . you know . . . afterward." A picture of him lying in the ditch flashed through my mind. I hadn't been able to move when it happened. I had just stood there, staring. Why hadn't I been able to help my best friend?

Kevin shrugged. "It doesn't matter now. What's done is done."

For a second I thought he'd been reading my mind, then I realized he was just answering his own question. "You're going to be okay, Kev."

"That's easy for you to say," he said quietly. "Nothing ever happened to you."

Just then I heard a rustling in the bushes, and Mrs. Kowalski came barreling through. "Kevin, why aren't you wearing your helmet? You know you're supposed to have it on whenever you walk any distance." Her skirt caught on some wild raspberry thorns and she yanked it loose, almost ripping the material.

"It's okay, Mom," Kevin said, "we were just . . ."

Mrs. Kowalski turned on me. "Didn't I warn you the other day? Didn't I tell you that anything might send him right back into the hospital?" She pulled Kevin to his feet and started leading him back toward the house, holding him up as if he had a sprained ankle or something.

"He walked fine all the way out here by himself, Mrs. Kowalski," I said, but she ignored me. I noticed Kevin had a little limp now, and he wasn't trying very hard to walk on his own. I followed along behind.

Kevin's father saw us coming and ran to meet us. "What's the matter? Is he hurt?"

Mr. Kowalski tried to take Kevin from her, but she shoved past him. "I can't leave him alone with you for five minutes, can I?"

Mr. Kowalski followed her. "But everything was fine a minute ago. What happened?"

"When he's outside he's supposed to be wearing his helmet. I told you that. Now I find him sitting down by the creek with his head bare! That's what happened!" She kept going toward the house.

"Sitting?" He stopped and turned to me. "What, you were just sitting? No broken bones?"

"No, sir. We were watching for frogs. Then Mrs. Kowalski came out and got all upset. I guess I shouldn't have taken him for a walk. I'm sorry."

"You didn't do anything wrong, Ryan."

Mr. Kowalski started running after them. "Greta, you're not helping Kevin by treating him like a baby."

She whirled around to face him. "Oh, and I suppose you're helping him by giving him no protection whatsoever." Kevin clung to his mother and buried his face in her shoulder like a little kid. I couldn't believe it. I'd never seen him do anything like that, even when we were little.

When Kevin looked up, he had tears streaming down his face. I couldn't stand it. I had to get out of there. As I took off down the street, I could still hear the Kowalskis yelling at each other.

Chapter 3

I heard Brenda in the kitchen with a couple of her friends when I got home, so I ducked in the front door and went right up to my room. I needed to be alone. Things weren't going the way I wanted them to anymore, and I needed time to think.

I dug through the junk on my desk until I found my old shoe box filled with pictures. I wanted to see Kevin the way he used to be. There were pictures of Kevin, Mooch, and me from the time we were in kindergarten. For a while we had looked like triplets, except for the hair. We always lost the same teeth at the same time. Then Kevin and I got taller and Mooch got wider.

While Mooch and I were standing like a couple of statues, saying "cheese," Kevin was always making faces or putting horns behind Mooch's head or mine. The best shot was the official group picture from scout camp last year. Kevin hid in a tree while our scout leader, Mr. Patton, got everybody lined up. Then, just as Mr. Patton snapped the shutter, Kevin swung down from a branch and hung upside down by his knees. Mr. Patton never noticed until the pictures were developed, and there was Kev, looking like a chimpanzee in a scout uniform.

I couldn't imagine him pulling off any great stunts like that again, at least not the way he was now. It made me sad, almost as if the Kevin I used to know had been killed that day on the bike.

"Ryan! Are you up there?" It was Mooch.

"Yeah," I yelled, "come on up."

"I told your dumb sister you must be here," he said, bursting into the room. "She said you were at Kevin's, but when I went over there, he said you went home."

"How was he?" I asked.

Mooch stretched out on my bed. "He looked as if he'd been crying. What did you do to him?"

"Nothing. Just had him go back to the creek with me." I told Mooch about what had happened with Mrs. Kowalski.

Mooch nodded. "Yeah, she got me out of there pretty fast, too. Doesn't want anybody to tire out her little baby."

"Maybe we should do something where Kevin can just sit. I could take over my new video game. That's not tiring."

"Why don't you and I just play it here?"

"What's the matter? You ready to give up on him already?"

Mooch shrugged. "No, I just don't want to deal with his mother again, that's all."

"Come on," I said, grabbing the game cassette. "We won't call first to give her a chance to say no."

We went through the back way. Mr. Kowalski was still working in his garden. "Hey Ryan," he said when he saw us, "I'm sorry about what happened before. Kevin's mother is still pretty upset about the accident. Maybe I shouldn't have let him go for a walk."

"That's okay, Mr. Kowalski," I said. "I brought over a computer game so we'd have something quiet to do."

"Good thinking. Can't see how his mother could object to that."

At first, Mrs. Kowalski wasn't too keen on us being there, but I think she was embarrassed about the scene she'd made before, so she let us in. "You can't stay all afternoon, though," she said. "I'm going to make Kevin take a nap in a little while."

Emily glared at us when we came into the living room. "How come Kevin can have friends over and I can't?"

"I told you," Mrs. Kowalski said, "we can't have

a lot of confusion in the house right now. The boys have just come to visit Kevin for a little while."

"How come Kevin's friends are visitors and my friends are confusion?"

Mrs. Kowalski left the room without answering her. Kevin was still in front of the TV.

"I just got Atom Smasher for my birthday," I said. "Want to try it? You, too, Emily. We can take turns."

Emily shrugged. "Sure. Why not?"

"This game is awesome," Mooch said, settling himself right in front of the computer screen. "So far, I hold the record for the most atoms smashed. You have to nail them before they blow up."

Mooch turned on Kevin's computer and loaded the game. He took his turn first so he could show Kevin how to play, then handed him the joystick. "Your turn," Mooch said.

"Let Emily go next," Kevin said. "I'll watch for a while."

Emily did pretty well, but she couldn't beat Mooch's score.

"You try it now, Kev," she said, handing the stick to him.

Kevin scrunched down in his seat. "It's supposed to be Mooch's turn."

"It doesn't matter. This is just practice," she said. "Besides, it's fun. Try it."

Kevin tried to move the smasher around after the atoms, but he wasn't fast enough. Two of them blew up right away. "I can't do this," Kevin said, letting go of the stick.

Emily sat on the couch next to Kevin. "Don't give up. You're just out of practice. It's not all that different from Pac Man, and you used to be a whiz at that."

"I used to be a whiz at a lot of things," Kevin mumbled.

Mooch moved in next to Kevin. "Try to get ahead of the atoms, Kev. Then they'll bump right into you and you can zap 'em before they get away."

Kevin finally got lined up on an atom, but he wasn't fast enough to smash it.

Mooch jumped up and grabbed the joystick. "Push the button, Kev. Don't just sit there like a dummy."

"Maybe that's what I am," Kevin said, flopping back against the pillows on the couch. "Go ahead, finish up my turn."

"You'll get the hang of it on the next round," I said. "It's just a matter of practice."

"Right," Kevin said, staring at the screen.

Mooch was really getting into it. As if the game didn't make enough noise on its own, he had to add his own sound effects. "Eeeeaaarrroooh . . . Pow!

Pow! Pow!" he yelled, knocking out three atoms in a row. "You're not getting away from me. Pow! Gotcha!"

Mrs. Kowalski came running into the room. "I thought you were going to do something quiet!"

Mooch kept playing, but clamped his teeth over his bottom lip to keep from yelling at the screen. There was no stopping him when he was on a roll.

Mrs. Kowalski brushed Kevin's hair out of his eyes and plumped up his pillows. Then she pushed the switch to turn off the game. Mooch still yanked at the joystick for a second or two until he realized the little green atoms had disappeared from the screen.

"This is too much excitement for Kevin," Mrs. Kowalski said. "You boys will have to leave so he can have his nap."

"Okay," I said. While Mrs. Kowalski was taking the joystick away from the dazed Mooch, I went over to Kevin. "Listen," I whispered, "we still need to talk about camp."

"Sure," Kevin said listlessly.

"No, really," I whispered. "I'll help you get ready. I'll convince your mother. We'll work on it together."

Kevin looked down at his lap. "Forget it. I'm not going."

"Nice work," I said to Mooch as we headed back down the road.

"What did I do?"

"You grabbed the stick away from Kev just as he was getting the hang of the game, for starters."

"He wasn't getting the hang of it. He was messing up."

"So you've never messed up? You have to give him a chance to do things on his own. You're as bad as his mother. And if you had kept your mouth shut, we'd still be there."

"I can't help it if I get a little carried away by video games," Mooch said. "At least I don't sit there like a corpse."

"That was a rotten thing to say, Mooch. You don't even care what happens to Kevin, do you?"

"Sure I do."

"You have a funny way of showing it," I said, kicking at a loose stone.

"Well, he's different now. He's not any fun."

"Give him a chance. He just got home."

Mooch stopped and looked at me. "You really think he's going to get back to the way he used to be?"

"Sure. Why not?"

"Because he got his head bashed in. That's why not. Wake up, Ryan."

"Okay, so he's a little different right now, but it's only been two months since his accident. My dad says that he's going to have therapy three times a week and with time, he'll get back to normal."

Mooch started off ahead of me. "Being with you and Kevin is about as exciting as watching grass grow. You never could think of any neat stuff to do."

I ran a few steps to catch up. "So? What neat stuff did you ever think of?"

"I never had to," Mooch said. "Kevin always did the thinking for both of us. All you ever say is, 'I don't know. What do you want to do?' "

I grabbed Mooch's arm. "Listen, the three of us have been best friends since kindergarten. Doesn't that count for something?"

Mooch stopped dead in his tracks. "It doesn't mean we're always going to be best friends, Ryan. People change, and they get new friends."

"Are you saying you don't want to be friends anymore?"

Mooch looked me in the eye. "All I know is I don't want to spend the whole summer sitting around trying to think of things to do. And I don't want to sit around waiting for Kevin to get back to being his old self again, because that's not going to happen. Maybe it's time for me to find some other kids to hang out with." From the look on his face, I could tell he meant it.

He turned away, and I watched his back as he trudged down the road. I couldn't believe it. Was I losing both of my best friends?

Chapter 4

"Why the long face?" Mom asked after supper.

"It's nothing," I said.

She peered at me over the top of the newspaper she was reading. "Does the 'nothing' have anything to do with Kevin?"

"I told you, everything's fine."

"Okay," Mom said, going back to her reading.

I flopped on the couch and clicked through thirty-two stations on the TV with the remote, but nothing looked good. I was halfway through the stations for the second time when Mom put down her paper. "Why don't you invite him to stay over tonight?"

"Who?"

"Kevin."

"Why?"

"I thought you'd enjoy it," she said. "Besides, it might be good for Kevin to get out for a change."

"You don't understand, Mom. Mrs. Kowalski

wouldn't let him stay over. She's been acting really weird lately."

"What do you mean, 'weird'?"

I told her about what had happened back at the creek, and at his house when we played Atom Smasher.

Mom thought for a minute. "I still think you should call him."

"His mother's just going to say no."

"So what? It wouldn't hurt to try. Besides, I'd like to see Kevin myself. I've missed having him around here."

"Okay, I'll call him."

"I'll check and see what we have in the way of snacks," Mom said, getting up. "If Mooch is coming, I'd better stock up."

"Who said anything about Mooch?"

Mom stopped in the doorway.

"You two have a fight?"

"I just don't feel like having him over, that's all."

I swear my mother can read my mind. The more I try to hide something from her, the better she can zero in on it.

As soon as Mom left the room, I dialed Kevin's number. His mother had to call him to the phone.

"Hello?"

"Hey, Kev, I just had a great idea. Want to sleep over tonight?"

"I don't know. I have to ask my mother."

"Okay, so go ask."

I could hear him asking her in the background. It sounded as if they were arguing about something. Then I could hear Kevin coming back into the room.

"She says I can't."

"Okay. Maybe another night."

"Yeah, maybe."

When I went into the kitchen, Mom was digging around in the cupboard for snacks. "So, what's the verdict?"

"Three guesses," I said, slumping into a kitchen chair.

She sat down across from me and tossed me an Oreo. "Too bad, but at least you gave it a shot."

"What's the matter with Mrs. Kowalski? Isn't it against the law to keep your kid a prisoner?"

Mom munched on her cookie. "I can understand how Greta feels. After all, she almost lost her son, and that has to be terrible. I'd probably be acting the same way if you were the one who got hurt. It's a shame, though. It would be good for Kevin to get out."

"Who was your best friend when you were a kid, Mom?"

Mom smiled. "I had two of them—Sally Kratz and Mary Ann Hinkle. We were inseparable."

"I never heard you talk about them."

"That's because I haven't heard from either of them in years. I think Mary Ann moved out of state."

"Did you have a fight?"

Mom fished another Oreo out of the bag.

"No, nothing like that. We just drifted apart in junior high. People change, you know."

Just then the phone rang, and I grabbed for it. It was Kevin. "I still can't come over, but you can sleep here if you want," he said.

"Great! I'll be right there. I'll bring Atom Smasher back and show you some of the fine points. Next time you'll beat Mooch easy."

"Whatever," Kevin said, and hung up.

Mom raised her eyebrows. "Was that who I think it was?"

"Yeah. He still can't come, but I can sleep over there, okay?"

"It's a step in the right direction. Maybe he can come over here next week. I'll talk to Greta about it the next time I see her."

I packed my backpack, told my parents good night, and headed for Kevin's. The sun had just gone down behind the woods, and the sky was streaked with pink and orange. I'm a sucker for a good sunset, so I sat down on a rock to watch.

Sunsets always get me thinking. If only Kevin and I hadn't gone riding that day. We could have done something else–anything else–instead. Then he'd still be his old wild self and things between him and Mooch and me would still be the same.

I thought about what Mom had said about Sally Kratz and Mary Ann Hinkle. Then I pictured Kevin, Mooch, and me in three boats without paddles, all drifting away from each other. I had to stop that from happening. So what if people change? That doesn't mean you can't go on being friends.

As the last few rays of pink faded from the sky, I picked up my stuff and went on to Kevin's. Emily was in the kitchen doing dishes when I knocked on the screen door. "Hi, Ryan. Kevin went to the store with Mom and Dad to get extra stuff for snacks, but they'll be back soon. I'm having Heather sleep over tonight, too."

"Okay, I'll give you a hand while I wait." I put down my backpack and started drying dishes.

Emily looked surprised, then smiled. "I wouldn't be having somebody over if you hadn't started the fight about Kevin sleeping at your house."

"I didn't mean to start a fight."

"Don't worry about it. Since Kevin's accident, the least little thing can start a fight around here. Anyway, Dad said Mom should let Kevin sleep over with you. Mom had a fit about that, so Dad came up with the plan about you coming here instead. Then he said it was only fair that if Kevin had a friend over, I should have one, too. So . . . thanks." She handed me a plate.

"How do you think Kevin's doing?" I asked.

"I think he's a lot better than he acts."

"You mean he's faking?"

Emily scrubbed at a pot. "Not really. It's just that Mom treats him like a piece of china. She has him convinced he can't do anything."

"Why's she doing that to him?"

"I don't know. Ever since the accident, all she thinks about is Kevin. She didn't have to quit her job and go out to Chicago with him."

"She didn't?"

"Not for the whole two months. The doctor here said Mom and Dad should go out for the first few days to get him settled, then go back and visit every other weekend or so. A lot of kids are out there without their parents. But Mom insisted on going. She and Dad had a big fight about it before she left."

"At least your dad is letting Kevin do a few things."

Emily wiped the counter and squeezed out the sponge. "He's not the one who usually wins around here, though." A car door slammed outside. "We can't talk anymore. They're back."

"Hi, Kev," I said as he came through the door, "I brought the game cartridge. Want to put it in the computer and learn to be an Atom Smasher champ?"

Kevin put a bottle of pop down on the table. "I'm pretty beat. Let's go up to my room."

"You don't go to bed this early, do you?" I asked.

Kevin glanced at the clock. "Not quite. I get pretty tired by this time of day though."

Just then Emily's friend arrived. "Come on," Kevin said, "I'm going upstairs."

He still didn't want to do anything when we got to his room. He stretched out on his bed and stared at the ceiling. I wandered around the room, looking for something to do. Kevin had last year's camp picture on his desk, as if he'd been looking at it. "Remember the neat trick we pulled off at camp last year?" I asked, picking up the picture.

"What trick?"

"You know—with the hamburgers."

"Oh, yeah," Kevin said, but from the expression on his face, I didn't think he remembered. It had been the greatest stunt anybody had ever pulled off at camp. Kevin convinced Mr. Patton to take us along when he went into town for supplies. Then he conned him into letting us stop at McDonald's. Mr. Patton thought we just wanted to get something to eat, but Kevin had a better plan. We spent every cent we'd brought to camp on hamburgers to go. Then we got back to camp and sold them to the other kids for twice what we paid for them. It didn't matter that they weren't hot by then. Even cold and greasy, they were still ten times better than the camp food. Everybody wanted one, and we doubled our money in ten minutes.

"Maybe we could do that again this year," I said. "We could get some cheeseburgers and fries this time, too."

Kevin scowled slightly, as if he were trying to remember.

"I bet we could charge even more," I said, trying to jog his memory without being obvious about it. "Those little kids were really desperate, remember? Their patrol had been having macaroni and cheese all week."

Suddenly Kevin sat up, grinning. "We ought to take candy from home this time," he said. "We could get candy bars three for a dollar at Super Duper and sell them for a buck apiece."

"What a great idea. Then we wouldn't have to count on Mr. Patton taking us into town again."

"Yeah," Kevin said. "He's probably wise to us now anyway. Maybe we should start buying the candy a little at a time and stash it away. Let's call Mooch and tell him about it."

This was the old Kevin talking. Now if he called Mooch, everything would be just like old times. Mooch would see that Kevin was going to be okay, and he wouldn't be mad anymore. "Go ahead," I said, "give him a call."

"You call," he said.

"Come on, Kev, the phone's right by your bed. You call him."

Kevin picked up the phone, started to dial, then hung up. "I forgot his number."

I couldn't figure out how he could forget a number he'd been calling all his life, but I gave it to him and he started dialing again. Then he stopped and looked at me. "What comes after the six?"

"Four," I said.

"Then what?"

I gave him the whole number again.

"I didn't ask for the whole number. All I wanted was what comes after the . . ."

"The what?"

"I don't know." He slammed down the receiver. "I can't do this. You call him."

"You mean you can't make a phone call anymore?"

Kevin flopped back on the pillow. "I can't keep the numbers straight in my head. Why do you think I didn't call you when I first got home?"

I pulled my chair closer to the bed. "Let me get this straight. You can't remember seven numbers long enough to dial a phone number?"

"Sure I can remember the numbers. I just can't

remember what order they go in." He grinned. "You get a lot of wrong numbers that way."

"Yeah, I can imagine. How did you call me tonight?"

"I didn't. Emily dialed your number for me after she called Heather."

I picked up the receiver. "Okay, don't worry about it. I'll call Mooch."

Kevin sat up. "Let's forget about calling Mooch tonight. We'll do something else instead."

"Sure," I said, "what do you want to do?"

Kevin stared across the room for a minute, then shrugged. "I don't know. What do *you* want to do?"

Chapter 5

Kevin slept forever the next morning. I banged around a little, hoping that might rouse him, but it didn't. My stomach was growling so loud, I'm surprised that didn't wake him up. Finally, I could hear Mrs. Kowalski coming up the stairs.

"Time to get up, sleepyheads. Your father thought you'd like to go to McDonald's for lunch."

Lunch? No wonder I was so hungry. "Sure, Mrs. Kowalski. Sounds great." I shook Kevin's arm. "Come on, Kev, wake up."

I slipped into my jeans and shirt and headed for the bathroom. When I came back out, Kevin was dressed and ready to go.

"That was fast," I said.

Kevin just shrugged.

The McDonald's in town was pretty crowded when we got there, but we found a couple of tables near the back where we could all fit. Mr. Kowalski and Emily went to get our food. We arrived just before the deadline on breakfast, so Kevin ordered pancakes.

Mrs. Kowalski put her arm around Kevin's shoulder. "How does it feel to be on your first outing?"

"Okay," Kevin said, but he just stared into space until his pancakes arrived. Then he speared one with his plastic fork and took a bite out of it.

"Kevin, for heaven's sake, let me cut those up for you," Mrs. Kowalski said, moving his plate in front of her.

Kevin grabbed the plate back. "I like eating them this way."

"Leave him alone, Mom," Emily said. "He always ate like a slob, even before the accident."

Mrs. Kowalski tried to ignore Kevin's table manners, but she was scowling as she ate.

There was a lot of noise at the front entrance as some of the guys from our class came in. Jeremy Schneider, last year's class president, spotted Kevin and came over to our table. A couple of the other kids followed.

"Hey, Kev," Jeremy said, "I didn't know you were back. How are you doing?"

Kevin put down the pancake he was devouring and grinned. "Great! Good as new."

"No kidding?" Jeremy said. "Boy, we were all worried about you."

The other kids joined in, asking Kevin questions about the accident, and about being in Chicago and stuff. I noticed they didn't ask me anything, but they were the class hotshots, and they'd never spoken much to me before. Kevin either for that matter, but now he was a big hero.

Kevin was really enjoying himself, but all of a sudden I noticed his mother looking at him funny. A big glob of pancake syrup was starting to drip off Kevin's lower lip. Suddenly Mrs. Kowalski reached over with her spoon, scraped up the syrup, and popped it into his mouth, as if he were a little baby who had dribbled his strained carrots. Jeremy stopped in mid-sentence and stared. So did the other guys.

"Well," Jeremy said, looking embarrassed, "we have to take off. We're going to a movie after we eat. Uh . . . see you."

"Yeah," I said, trying to cover up the awkward silence, "see you."

"Did you have to do that?" Kevin said quietly when they had gone.

Mrs. Kowalski smiled. "Do what?"

"Forget it." Kevin got up and headed for the rear door.

"What's gotten into him?" Mrs. Kowalski asked.

"You just made him look like a jerk in front of his friends, that's all," Emily said. "Why don't you leave him alone?"

Mrs. Kowalski started to get up. "Oh, I feel terrible. I was so used to feeding him those first few weeks after the accident, I just didn't think . . ."

Mr. Kowalski reached out and stopped her. "Sit down and finish your meal, Greta. Kevin will be all right."

"I'm finished," I said, hiding the last of my burger in my napkin. "I'll go outside and wait with him."

Kevin was slumped down in the backseat of the car. I slid in next to him. "Don't get all bent out of shape, Kev. I'm sure nobody noticed what your mom did."

"Right," Kevin mumbled, "that's why they tripped over each other trying to get away from me."

"So who needs those kids anyway? They all think they're such big shots."

"Who are you trying to kid?" Kevin mumbled. "They *are* big shots."

Kevin was pretty quiet after we got home. I kept trying to come up with ideas of things to do, but he just wanted to watch TV. Finally, I gave up and got ready to leave. I thanked the Kowalskis for having me over. "Maybe next time Kevin can stay at my house," I said.

Mr. Kowalski slapped me on the back. "I was just thinking the same thing, Ryan. It's a deal."

As I took off through the back field, Emily was sitting up on a branch of the tree at the end of the Kowalskis' yard.

"Mind if I come up?" I asked.

"Help yourself."

I climbed to the branch opposite her. "We've got to do something about Kevin. He needs to get away from your mom for a while."

Emily picked at a piece of bark. "Fat chance of that happening. You saw what she's like."

"Well, he's supposed to go to scout camp with us next month. Maybe things will be better after that."

"Mom isn't going to let him go."

"Do you know that for sure?" I asked, shifting around for a more comfortable spot on my tree limb. "Has she said something?"

"Yeah. She and Dad had a big fight about it yesterday. She says Kevin wouldn't be able to take care of himself at camp, and he wouldn't be able to do any of the things the other kids do."

"That's stupid," I said. "Kevin can do a lot more than she gives him credit for."

Emily dropped down and swung from her branch by her hands. "Tell me about it!" she said, landing on the ground. "Now that Kevin's so helpless, I'm the official family slave." She started back toward the house.

"Wait a minute," I called, jumping down and following her. "If I could come up with a plan to make Kevin do more, would you help me?"

Emily turned around. "What are you—some kind of magician?"

"What if I got him away for a couple of days on a camping trip? It wouldn't have to be far away. Maybe just back in the woods."

Emily snorted. "In your dreams, Ryan. Mom wouldn't let him camp out in our backyard."

"Maybe she wouldn't have to know."

"What are you going to do? Kidnap her and tie her up someplace?"

"No," I said slowly, as a plan formed in my mind, "but I might kidnap Kevin."

Emily came closer. "Ryan, that's the stupidest idea I ever heard."

"That's what they told Columbus when he said the world was round, and look how that turned out."

"Yeah, he found the wrong continent."

Mrs. Kowalski called from the back porch. "Emily! You didn't finish the dishes from last night!"

"Didn't you and Kevin used to take turns with the dishes?" I asked.

Emily bent down to pick up her cat. "Yeah. Now I get stuck with them all myself."

"You want that to go on the rest of your life?"

"Emily!" Mrs. Kowalski shouted. "Answer me when I call you."

"I'll be there in a few minutes, Mom." Emily turned to me. "Okay, I'll try anything. How are we going to do it?"

"I could set up a campsite back in the woods. It wouldn't even have to be that far in. We could tell your parents he was sleeping over at my house."

Emily bit her lip. "Dad would probably go along with that. It would only work for one night, though."

"Okay, even if we just camped overnight, I think I could show Kevin he's better than he thinks he is."

"But how are you going to get him into the woods in the first place?" She set the cat back down on the ground, and it rubbed against my legs.

"I'll have to figure that out. I don't think I could get him to walk in."

"And another thing," Emily said, "what if something happens to Kevin while you're back in the woods with him? There's a lot of stuff you haven't thought of, Ryan."

"Give me a break! I'm just working things out in my mind. There need to be two people in the woods with Kevin—one to stay with him while the other one goes for help if we need it."

"I could go along with you."

"No, I need you to cover at home and keep your mother from getting suspicious."

"Okay, I'll help, but just make sure you have a good plan before you go dragging Kevin off into the woods. You could make things worse instead of better."

As much as I hated to admit it, Emily was right. I needed another person to make the plan work, and the only one I could think of was Mooch.

Chapter 6

I worked on my plan the whole next day, then called Mooch the following morning. He didn't sound too interested in seeing me until I mentioned that my mother had just baked a batch of double chocolate brownies. That got him.

"I wasn't sure you'd want to come," I said, after Mooch had eaten his fourth brownie.

"Why not?" he asked, chewing.

"Well, you said something about finding somebody else to hang out with."

Mooch shrugged. "Didn't get around to it yet."

"Listen, Mooch, I could really use your help with Kevin. I'm not talking about a big deal here. Just a couple of days to set things up. I think we could get Kev back to being his old self again."

"How?"

I took a deep breath and launched into my plan,

but Mooch didn't let me get past the word "kid-nap."

"What are you, crazy?" he yelled. "You can go to jail for that!"

I ran over and closed my door. "Keep it down, will you? You want my whole family to hear you?"

"Yeah, so they can talk you out of it. It's a dumb idea, Ryan. You just can't go around kidnapping people. They send in the FBI for stuff like that."

I handed him another brownie. "That's when you kidnap somebody for ransom. What we're doing is for Kevin's own good. Just let me explain what I want to do."

"I don't want to hear this, because then I'll be in trouble just from knowing about it."

"You're right, but it's too late. You already know about the kidnapping, so you're as guilty as I am. You might as well hear the rest."

"That's not fair," Mooch said, stuffing the brownie into his mouth. "I'm innocent."

"Oh yeah? Just try telling that to the FBI." I pulled my chair over close to the bed so I wouldn't have to talk loud. "Kevin's never going to get any better with his mother around. She's treating him like a baby."

"So? How does kidnapping him make him get better?"

"He can already do more than he thinks. I'm sure

of it. He's just scared to try anything, and his mother is making him that way. If we get him away from her, we can prove to him that he's going to be okay."

"Where are we going to hide him?" I noticed that Mooch had changed from "you" to "we" at this point, so I figured I was winning him over.

"We'll set up a camp back in the woods. That way, we can work on the things that Kevin has to learn to do before camp."

"Hide in the woods? Oh sure. The FBI will track us down in the first half hour."

"Not if nobody knows we're gone. We'll tell our parents we're sleeping over at each other's houses."

"Be real, Ryan. Mrs. Kowalski isn't going to let Kevin sleep over with either one of us."

"That's all taken care of. Mr. Kowalski practically promised he could stay over with me."

"Yeah, but Mrs. Kowalski would be coming over here once an hour to see how Kevin was doing."

"That's where Emily comes in. She's going to keep her mother distracted so she doesn't get suspicious."

Mooch's eyes widened. "You told Emily about this? She'll blab the whole thing."

"No, she won't. She wants Kevin to get better as much as anybody."

"They're going to find us easy," Mooch said, grabbing another brownie.

"That's the beauty of it. They won't even know we're missing. Besides, they couldn't find us even if they were looking. Remember the hunter who got lost in the woods a few years ago? He walked in circles for two days and came out way over on County Line. There must be hundreds of acres of trees. Most people don't know their way around in there like we do. Not even our parents."

Mooch looked interested. "We could set up a real campsite, couldn't we?"

"Sure, and Kevin would be fine, once we got him back there."

Mooch polished off the last of the brownies. "Okay, let's give it a shot."

First we had to find a spot for the campsite. Mooch's house was the second one down the road from Kevin's, and I lived next door to Mooch. Each house had a back field that ran all the way to the creek with a bridge to the woods on the other side. We lived in old farmhouses, and they were set pretty far apart, not close together like new houses are. There was a thick hedgerow along each property line, so you couldn't see from one yard to another.

The Manuses' bridge had rotted away years ago, but we still had a good one and so did the Lockwoods, the people who lived between Mooch and Kevin. The Lockwoods were away on vacation, so we decided to use their bridge. That way nobody could see us from Kevin's house or Mooch's. The Lockwoods' path went about a quarter of a mile back from the creek to the point where the woods opened up. There was an area of thick underbrush about a half mile back from that.

"This is the perfect spot," I said. "We can hide the tent under that brush. It's just like a book I read once. These two guys were hiding out in the mountains, so they covered up their tent and gear with branches. When the bad guys came looking for them, they went right by without stopping."

Mooch slapped at a mosquito. "They didn't have the FBI coming after them. And *we're* the bad guys, Ryan. Did you ever stop to think of that?"

"The point is that it worked," I said. "Besides, we're not bad guys. We're only trying to help a friend."

We had just started clearing a space big enough for the tent in the middle of the clump of brush, when Mooch sat down.

"Don't take a break yet, Mooch. We'll never get this place ready at the rate you're going."

Mooch folded his arms. "This isn't going to work."

"Why not?"

"Kevin will never be able to walk this far," Mooch said, "and I'm sure not going to carry him."

"Okay, so he can't walk in here. Maybe we could pull him in a wagon."

"Are you crazy? Pull him over all those rocks and branches? That path isn't exactly like a sidewalk, you know. It would take a team of mules to get him back here. Besides, what makes you think he'd want to come into the woods in the first place?"

I sat down next to Mooch. "All right, let's not panic. There has to be some way to get Kevin back here."

"I know!" Mooch said. "I saw this neat-o movie once, where a bunch of Indians strapped a wounded guy to a couple of logs and tied the other end of the logs to a horse and then dragged him across the prairie to get to a doctor."

"Brilliant. As soon as we find two logs and steal a horse, we're all set."

Mooch picked up his hatchet. "Okay, I'll start cutting down trees, and you . . ."

"I was kidding! You don't think the neighbors would notice us dragging a screaming kid behind a hot horse?"

"Oh," Mooch said, dropping the hatchet, "yeah. Then how about my brother's four-wheel all-terrain vehicle? Kevin's always wanted to ride on that."

"Don't be stupid. Gary would never let us use his four-wheeler."

"He won't have to know. He goes to work first thing every morning, and I could have it back before he got home."

"You mean you know how to drive it?"

"Sure. Piece of cake."

"That's perfect. Kevin won't need any convincing at all to ride on the four-wheeler." The plan was complete.

It took us three more days to get the campsite set up. We had to do it a little at a time, so nobody would get suspicious. Each day we stopped over at Kevin's for a little while, so I could drop another hint about him staying over. It also gave me a chance to fill Emily in on what we were doing.

When everything else was ready, we took in the food. I scrounged as much stuff as I could without my mother noticing. I packed three cans of baked beans and what was left of the bag of Oreos for supper, and some doughnuts and a box of Cheerios for breakfast. For lunch the next day, I put in three old packages of backpacking meals that were left over from a trip Brenda took on the Appalachian Trail last summer. Mooch brought Kool-Aid and a couple of gallon jugs of water.

We had put my family's four-man tent in the middle of the brush, and put the branches that we cut over the top for camouflage. You had to crawl through a little tunnel to get to the tent opening.

Mooch grinned. "Got to hand it to you, Ryan. You'd never even notice this tent was here, unless you were looking for it."

"Yeah, it turned out even better than I thought it would," I said, looking around. "Did you set up your alibi with your mother?"

"I told her I'd be at your house tonight. Don't worry about her calling, though. She never does."

"Okay. My mom thinks I'm at your house. I don't think she'll call either. She never has when I've slept over before." I pulled one last branch over the top of the tent. "Come on. It's time to invite Kevin for the sleepover."

Mooch grinned. "Some sleepover!"

Emily was out back in her tree when we went to Kevin's house.

"You sit up there to spy on us?" Mooch asked.

Emily looked ready to spit on Mooch's head. "I sit up here so I can look down on you, nerd."

"Never mind him, Emily," I said. "This is it! We have the camp all set up. Now all we have to do is convince your mother to let him stay over tonight."

Emily jumped down from the tree and started walking toward the house with us. "Dad's been working on her, so I think she'll say yes. I just hope

I can handle her. How long are you going to be gone?"

I looked at my watch. "It's three o'clock. If we can go right away, we'll have time to do quite a bit this afternoon. Then we'll have an early breakfast in the morning, do some more stuff, and get back by noon. Just don't let your mom come over or call before that."

Kevin was watching the tube as usual when we went into the house. His mother was with him. "Hi, Mrs. Kowalski," I said, "my mom wanted to know if Kevin could spend the rest of the day at our house and sleep over tonight."

She looked at me funny. I knew it! She could tell I was lying. She was using that mind-reading device that mothers have. "That's nice of your mother, Ryan. As a matter of fact she talked to me about Kevin staying over when I saw her at the supermarket yesterday."

Mooch's mouth fell open. "She did?"

I stuck my elbow in Mooch's ribs. "That's great. So it's all set then, right?"

Mrs. Kowalski bit her lip. "Well, if you're sure you're not going to do anything strenuous . . ."

"We won't," I said. It wasn't a lie. After all, Kevin was getting a ride all the way into the woods. How strenuous was that?

"All right." Mrs. Kowalski smiled. "I'll go upstairs and get some things ready for you, Kevin."

Emily winked at me. A few minutes later Mrs. Kowalski came back downstairs with a suitcase big enough for a three-week trip.

"Just remember not to overdo, dear," she said. "Shall I drive you down to Ryan's house?"

"Aw, Mom," Kevin said, "I can walk that far."

Mrs. Kowalski handed Kevin his helmet. "All right, but I'll call before bedtime to check on you."

Mooch went on ahead with Kevin, and I got Emily alone in the backyard. "You've got to keep her from calling. If she does, we're in big trouble."

"Don't worry. I'll keep her busy this afternoon, then I'll get her to take me to Marketplace Mall tonight. I'll just make sure we stay out past Kevin's bedtime, so she won't be able to call."

"You sure that will work?"

"You have any better ideas?"

"Not really. Good luck!"

Emily smiled. "You, too."

I ran to catch up to Mooch and Kevin. They were almost across the Lockwoods' field.

"Let's go back to the creek and mess around for a while," I said when I caught up to them.

"Shouldn't we take my stuff in the house first?" Kevin asked.

"Leave it over there under the bush," I said. "Nobody's going to take it. The Lockwoods aren't even home. We can pick it up on the way back. Hey, Mooch, why don't you go get the surprise to show Kevin."

"What surprise?" Kevin asked.

Mooch looked puzzled. "Yeah, what surprise?"

"You know," I said, holding out my arms as if I were hanging onto the handlebars of the four-wheeler.

"Oh, *that* surprise," Mooch said. "I'll be right back with it."

"What's he getting?" Kevin asked.

"You'll see in a minute."

Suddenly there was a loud coughing and sputtering. At least Mooch knew how to start the four-wheeler. Now if he only knew how to drive it. Nobody was home at his house this time of day, but the whole neighborhood could hear him. There was a small opening in the hedgerow near the creek. I sure hoped Mooch knew how to steer.

I ran over to the opening in the bushes. It didn't look like Mooch was heading for it. Not only that, he wasn't even slowing down, and he was getting closer by the second. Before I could yell for him to watch out, he buried the front end of the four-wheeler in the bushes. The engine sputtered and stopped.

Kevin almost ran over to the hedgerow. "What's going on? What was that noise?"

"Uh . . . this is the surprise, Kev. Mooch is going to take us for a ride in the woods."

"Are you crazy?" Kevin asked, backing up.

"I thought you knew how to drive that thing," I said.

Mooch picked some burdocks off his socks. "I do, but I didn't say I knew how to stop it."

"Is it wrecked?" Kevin asked.

"Naw. Gary drove it into a tree once, and it was okay. These bushes are soft. Didn't even scratch it. So . . . you want a ride, Kev?"

"With you driving? No thanks!"

"Come on," I said, "you've been dying to ride on one of these. When will you get another chance?"

Kevin eyed the red machine as Mooch started it up again and backed it out. "Well . . . maybe just a short ride."

"Sure. We'll have you back in no time," I said, feeling a little guilty about lying to him. "You sit behind Mooch. I'll climb on the back." Mooch handed me the extra helmet.

As soon as we got on board, Mooch slammed the four-wheeler into gear and we took off. "All right!" Kevin yelled, as we bounced and lurched across the Lockwoods' field toward the bridge. He sounded like the old Kevin again. The plan was working already.

Chapter 7

"Slow down, Mooch!" I yelled over Kevin's shoulder. "We're getting pretty close to the bridge."

"Whad'ya say, Ryan?" I could barely hear Mooch over the roar of the engine, and he didn't seem to be able to hear me at all with his helmet on. The four-wheeler was heading full speed toward the Lockwoods' bridge, but Mooch was aiming too far to the right.

"Steer, will you?" I shouted, but it was too late. I grabbed Kevin as I felt the front end of the four-wheeler dip over the creek bank. Fountains of water sprang up on both sides of us and about sixteen frogs shot out of the creek like cannonballs.

"Hang on," Mooch yelled, "I think I missed the bridge."

"No kidding," I shouted back, ducking as the water came down on our heads. "I thought it was a sudden rainstorm."

Luckily, the creek was shallow, and the four-wheeler kept going. Mooch gunned the engine, and we roared up the opposite creek bank.

Kevin let out a whoop. "That was better than the water slide at Darien Lake!"

Somehow Mooch managed to keep the four-wheeler on the path until we came to the point where the woods opened up. This was where most people started getting lost. There was no path from now on, only acre after acre of tall maple trees. One looked pretty much like another, unless you knew what to watch for. We'd played out here all our lives, so we could recognize a certain rock, or the way a particular branch twisted around. Mooch followed our secret landmarks back into the woods, then lurched to a stop by a maple tree with a double trunk. Just beyond was the section of thick underbrush with our tent hidden somewhere under it.

I slid off the back of the four-wheeler. "Shall we show Kevin our surprise?"

"What surprise?" Mooch asked. I gave him an elbow in the ribs. Mooch has a memory like a sieve. "Oh, sure, *that* surprise. Wait till you see it, Kev."

"See what?" Kevin reached out for me to help him off the seat, but I looked the other way. When I turned back, he had gotten off by himself. He was getting better already.

"Follow us," I said.

Kevin wasn't so good at walking over branches and vines. "I can't go in there," he said, "I'm going to trip."

I picked up a branch about the size of a cane. "Here, use this to keep your balance." I handed it to him, then turned away and kept walking.

Mooch went on ahead, planting himself by the entrance to the tunnel. "Ta-da! Welcome to Camp Manuse."

I caught up to him. "Where do you get off calling it after yourself?" I whispered. "I was the brains behind this operation."

"All right—Camp Manuse-Zeigler, then."

"Camp Zeigler-Manuse."

"What camp? Where?" Kevin asked, trying to get his foot loose from a vine. "I'm caught. Get me out of this thing."

"Sure, Kev." Mooch started toward Kevin, but I stopped him.

"You can do it, Kev. You wouldn't have anybody to get you untangled from vines if you were at scout camp."

"Sure I would. I'd have you guys."

"Yeah," Mooch said, "we'd all be together and we'd be able to . . ." Mooch stopped when I shot him a look.

"If you want to see our camp, you'd better get yourself loose," I said. "Come on." I shoved Mooch

ahead of me into the tunnel. I could hear Kevin
thrashing away at the vines as we crawled through
to the tent.

"Why are you being so mean to him, Ryan? He's
not acting like this on purpose. He really can't do a
lot of stuff anymore."

"I know that, but we can't baby him like his
mother does. We've got to prove to Kevin that he's
better than he thinks he is, and we don't have much
time to do it."

Mooch shook his head. "I'm not so sure this was
a good idea."

"It's the only chance Kevin has. Now, you've got
to get the four-wheeler back. And grab Kevin's suitcase on your way into the woods."

"In case somebody sees me, where am I supposed to be? I can't remember."

"Geez, Mooch, we've been over this a dozen
times. It depends who you run into. Kevin's family and your mother think we're all at my house.
But my family thinks I'm sleeping over with you.
Just don't let anybody see you on the four-
wheeler."

Mooch scratched his head. "I don't know, Ryan,
this is getting too complicated."

"Shhh . . . listen! Kevin's crawling through the
tunnel. As soon as he gets here, you sneak out and
carry through with the plan. Deal?"

Mooch shrugged and let out a sigh.

"We've got to do this for Kevin," I said.

"Okay. For Kevin."

Just then, Kevin pulled himself into the tent. "Far out! When did you guys do this?"

"We've been working on it the past few days," I said, watching Mooch slip behind Kevin and into the tunnel. "Pretty neat, huh?"

Kevin looked around. "Yeah, it's great. Have you been sleeping out here?"

"Not yet. We're going to, though. Want to camp out with us?"

"Yeah, sure . . ." Kevin's smile faded. "No, I'd better not."

"Come on, Kev, it'll be good practice for camp." I dug into my gym bag and pulled out two pairs of jeans. "Let's get out of our wet clothes. These should fit you." I tossed the jeans to him, but Kevin didn't even try to catch them.

"That's okay, I don't need to change." There was a sudden roar as Mooch started up the four-wheeler. Kevin jumped. "Where's Mooch going?"

"He's . . . uh . . . going to gather up some dry wood. Then we can have a campfire and pretend we're at Massawepie."

"This is about as close as I'm ever going to get to camp again," Kevin mumbled. He started to sit on my sleeping bag.

"Come on, Kev, put on the dry jeans, will you? You're going to get my sleeping bag all wet."

I changed my clothes, then looked over at Kevin. He was still trying to get his jeans open.

"What's the matter? Can't you get your pants undone?"

Kevin shook his head and let his hands fall to his sides.

"You're not even trying, Kev."

"I can't."

"What do you mean? You got dressed the morning I stayed over. Or did your mother help you . . . that's it, isn't it?"

"Knock it off, Ryan." Kevin started fumbling with the pants again. "I can do the zipper. It's just the snap that I can't . . ." He yanked hard and the snap popped open.

"Can't what?"

"Never mind," Kevin said, pulling off the pants.

I went over to the corner of the tent and pretended to be sorting out the food. I could hear Kevin struggling to get into my jeans, but I waited until I thought he was finished. When I turned around again, Kevin had the jeans on, but the fly was still undone. "That's attractive," I said. "You planning on going around for the rest of the day like a flasher?"

"I'll have Mom or Dad fix them when I get home."

"Will you come off it and stop being such a baby?" I yelled. "Never mind camp. You won't even be able to go back to school, if you don't shape up."

"Maybe I don't want to go back to school."

"What are you going to do? Veg out the rest of your life? Just sit and stare at the tube every day?"

Kevin plunked himself down on my sleeping bag and stared at the wall of the tent. "Maybe," he said in a flat voice, "maybe that's just what I'm going to do." His eyes were starting to fill up with tears.

This was going to be harder than I'd planned. I had to get out of the tent. I walked far enough away so I couldn't hear Kevin crying. It sounded like fake crying anyway, as if he wanted me to hear him and feel sorry for him. Well, that might work with his mother, but it wasn't going to work with me. Just thinking about it made me mad. I smashed my fist into a tree trunk. It hurt so bad I had to bite my tongue to keep from crying myself.

I decided not to push Kevin any more until Mooch got back. I figured he'd be embarrassed to act like a baby with both of us there. After a while Kevin's crying stopped, and I heard some heavy breathing and twigs cracking. Mooch was back.

"Did you put the four-wheeler back where you found it?" I asked.

"Yeah. I even made it over the bridge this time. All I needed was a little practice."

"Too bad you didn't have a little practice before you brought us out here. Do you think anybody saw you?"

Mooch shook his head. "The whole neighborhood was dead. We're safe."

"Why did you bring my suitcase here?" Kevin asked, crawling out of the tunnel opening. As he stood up, I noticed he'd managed to fasten his pants.

"I thought you'd need some stuff if you were going to camp out, so I went back for it." Mooch handed him the suitcase.

"I told you," Kevin said, "I can't."

I put my hands on Kevin's shoulders. "Look, Kev, I don't want you to get all bent out of shape about this, but we planned this whole thing ahead of time."

"Planned what?"

"We kidnapped you!" Mooch said, grinning. "Just like in the movies."

"Knock it off, guys," Kevin said, sitting down on a stump. "Let's go back. I'm getting tired."

"That's what I was trying to tell you," I said. "We're really camping out tonight. You'd like that, wouldn't you?"

"Well sure, but if my mom found out . . ."

"She's not going to find out," Mooch said. "She thinks you're sleeping over at Ryan's, remember?"

He went over to the tent and started crawling through the tunnel.

Kevin started toward the tent, then turned to me.

"But Mom is going to check up on me and find out I'm not at your house."

"Emily's in on this, too," I said. "She's covering for us."

Kevin looked puzzled. "Emily? But why?"

"I asked her to. We all knew your mother wouldn't let you come back here."

Kevin sat down on a log. "Why didn't you let me in on what you were doing earlier? You didn't have to kidnap me."

"Would you have said yes if we'd asked you?"

Kevin thought for a minute. "Probably not."

"But now that you're here, you're glad, right?"

Kevin looked around. "Yeah, this is pretty neat."

Mooch came out of the tunnel with the backpack of food. "I don't know about you guys, but I'm starved. Isn't it time for dinner?"

"By the time we build a fire, it will be," I said. "Let's gather up some wood."

We cleared an area and laid a lean-to fire the way we'd been taught in scouts. Kevin even helped a little, but he kept looking at us funny, as if he didn't quite trust us.

"Okay, you guys," I said, "each one of us gets his own can of beans."

"How are we supposed to cook them?" Mooch asked.

I'd forgotten about bringing a pan, but I tried to cover. "We'll just put the cans in the fire. The beans will get cooked okay."

Kevin wrinkled his nose. "Are you kidding? They'll get all burned on the bottom."

"Never mind, I'll eat mine cold." Mooch grabbed a can and opened it. "We have cold beans for dinner a lot at home."

He handed the can opener to Kevin, but Kevin pushed it away. "You'd better do mine, Mooch."

"Oh, sure, Kev."

"Don't touch his can of beans," I said, moving between them. "If you want to eat, Kev, you're going to have to open that can yourself."

"Aw, come on, Ryan, give the kid a break, will you?"

"He doesn't need a break. He needs to learn to do things by himself."

"But just let me give him a hand with . . ."

Kevin grabbed the can opener back from Mooch. "It's okay, Mooch, I can do it." He sat down on the ground with the can of beans on a flat rock in front of him.

You had to squeeze the handles of the can opener with your left hand while you turned the crank with the right. I watched Kevin struggle with it. He couldn't squeeze hard enough with his left hand and the opener kept slipping off the rim of the can.

"See? I knew he couldn't do it," Mooch whispered.

Maybe I was being too hard on Kevin. After all, he seemed to be trying. "Look," I said, "try it the other way around. Your right hand is the strongest, so squeeze with that and reach over with your left hand to turn the crank." I squatted down and showed Kevin what I meant, but he barely even tried. He just poked at the crank a few times with his left hand and gave up, sulking.

"Well, I hope you had a big lunch," I said, standing up, "because you're going to get pretty hungry without supper. I'll make the Kool-Aid. You better have that can of beans open when I come out of the tent."

I took my time, because I knew it wouldn't be easy for Kevin to get the can open. I wasn't sure what I would say or do if he hadn't managed it.

When I came back out of the tent, Kevin was eating from his open can of beans. "Hey, you did it! That's great."

Kevin kept eating and didn't look up.

"No kidding, Kev," I said, punching him on the arm. "Doesn't it make you feel good to do something you didn't think you could do?"

Suddenly Kevin struggled to his feet and threw

his can of beans into the brush. "Just get off my back, will you?" He headed back toward the path, limping as his left heel pulled up with each step.

Mooch was pretending to concentrate on his beans. I grabbed the neck of his T-shirt. "You opened it for him, didn't you?"

Mooch twisted out of my grip. "So, I gave him a little help. What's the big deal?"

"He won't do anything if you don't stick to the plan." I ran after Kevin. "I'm sorry, Kev. I just want you to . . ."

Kevin turned to face me. "Where's the four-wheeler? I want to go home."

"Mooch had to take it back before his brother discovered it was missing. The only way to get home is by walking, and we're three-quarters of a mile from the creek."

Kevin's face crumpled.

"Look, don't start crying again, Kev, it's going to be okay."

Kevin sat down on a log and put his head in his hands. Mooch came running over and pulled me aside. "Geez! What did you do to him now?"

"Nothing. I just told him he'd have to walk to get out of here."

"Knock it off, will you? You're just making things worse by pointing out all the stuff he can't do."

I looked over at Kevin. He wiped his eyes on his

sleeve and stared off into the woods. "Maybe you're ready to give up on him, Mooch," I said, "but I'm not."

I went over to Kevin. "Look, I'm going to tell you what's really going on here. Mooch and I thought you needed to get away from home so you could start doing more for yourself."

Kevin wiped his nose on his other sleeve. "Is that why you're acting like a Marine drill sergeant?"

I sat down on the log next to him and started writing my name in the dirt with a stick. "I guess I sounded rotten back there. I just want you to get better, that's all."

Kevin picked up a stick and erased my name. "You have a funny way of showing it. So this isn't just camping out in the woods, is it? You're going to put me through some kind of a test."

"It's not a test. It's a chance for you to see how much you can do without your mother rushing in to help you every other minute. All you need to do is try, Kev. Don't keep asking us to do everything for you. Your mom's been treating you like a baby."

"Don't blame her. She had to. You didn't see me in the hospital, Ryan. I was really banged up. I could hardly move."

"That was then. This is now."

Kevin didn't say anything for a few minutes.

"This could be like a trial run for scout camp," I

said. "If you can make it here, your mother will have to let you go."

"You mean we're going to tell her about what we've done?"

"Sure, after we get back. She may be a little mad at first, but after we explain why we did it, she'll be okay."

"I don't know, Ryan." More silence from Kevin, but I could tell he was thinking it over.

"What do you say, Kev? Are you willing to take a chance so you can go to camp with us?"

Kevin looked up. "Okay, I'll try. But quit being such a grouch, will you?"

"Deal," I said. "Come on, let's go find your beans. It's a long time until breakfast."

Chapter 8

"I always wondered what these woods looked like at night," Mooch said.

The woods didn't seem like the old familiar place we'd always known, now that the sun had gone down. The trees right around the campsite glowed orange from the firelight, but beyond that was total blackness. Anything could be hiding out there, and we'd never know about it. I shivered from the dampness and poked a stick into the fire to keep it going.

"What did you expect? The woods look dark."

"No, I mean I thought it would be scary. It's not. It's just . . . it's just . . ."

"Dark," Kevin said.

"Yeah, dark," Mooch said. He took a long drink from the plastic jug of Kool-Aid, then shuddered as he handed it to Kevin. "I really hate lime."

Kevin took a swig. "Yeah, it's gross. It tastes like

the junk my mother uses to wash the kitchen floor."

"You drink the stuff your mother uses on the floor?" Mooch poked Kevin in the ribs, making him splurt Kool-Aid down the front of his shirt.

Kevin grinned. "It just smells like this stuff tastes."

Mooch looked over his shoulder. "Anyway, I thought it would be scary in the dark here. There must be all kinds of dead bodies buried in these woods."

Kevin sat up straighter. "Bodies? From what?"

"I don't know. From way back. Didn't Indians and settlers live here? They're probably buried all around us."

"They put dead people in cemeteries and burial grounds," I said. "They didn't just plant them where they dropped."

Mooch jutted out his chin, making his jaw look huge in the firelight. "Were you there, Ryan? Is that what makes you such an expert about what happened to the Indians and settlers?"

Kevin snorted.

"No, really," Mooch said. "Did you ever notice how Ryan always thinks he knows more than anybody else?"

"That's because I read books, which is more than I can say for the rest of the people in these woods."

Mooch folded his arms. "I don't care. I still say

there are bodies back here. Maybe even ghosts."

"Ghosts?" Kevin's eyes widened. "You really think so?"

"Will you two cut it out? You're going to scare yourselves to death."

Kevin grabbed my arm, and I practically jumped out of my skin. "Shhh!" he whispered. "What was that?"

"What was what?"

"I just heard something."

I pulled my arm out of his grip. "It was probably just some animal."

"Yeah," Mooch said, starting to get up, "like a wolf. I bet that's what it is—a wolf. Quick, we gotta douse the fire."

Kevin pulled him back. "That's the worst thing you can do. If it's a wolf, the fire will keep it away."

"Calm down," I said. "When was the last time either of you heard about a wolf running loose in Ontario, New York?"

"We have foxes, don't we?" Mooch said. "How different is a fox from a wolf?"

"Very!" I couldn't believe these two. They were working themselves up into a panic over nothing. Then I heard it, too. But it wasn't an animal. "Voices! Somebody's coming!"

Mooch jumped to his feet. "It's the FBI. What did I tell you, Ryan?"

"Dummy up, Mooch. Come on, let's put this fire out." Mooch poured the rest of our Kool-Aid over the flames. We all stamped on the sizzling coals, bumping into each other.

"I smell smoke," a deep voice said. "Somebody's got a fire back here."

"Quick! Get to the tent," I whispered. We started for the tunnel, but Kevin fell. After staring into the fire for so long, it was almost impossible to see anything in the dark.

"Look," Mooch said, "there's a whole bunch of them coming!" About half a dozen flashlight beams were bobbing around, heading our way. Mooch freaked. "We're dead for sure! They'll shoot first and ask questions later."

I felt something grab my leg. It was Kevin. "Who's going to shoot? Why do they want us?"

"Where the heck are you, Kev?" I groped around by my feet and found his shoulder. "Come on, get up."

"I can't."

Mooch and I got on each side of Kevin and hauled him to his feet. The voices and flashlights were getting closer. I couldn't let them catch us now. Kevin wasn't ready. He'd go right back to the way he'd been with his mother.

We stumbled over to where I thought the tunnel

was, dragging Kevin between us. "I can't see a thing. Can you feel the opening, Mooch?"

"Hang on to Kevin. I'll look." We could hear Mooch thrashing around.

"Who's out there?" Kevin whispered. "Why are they after us?"

"It's the FBI," Mooch whispered. "I told you Emily would blab about the kidnapping, Ryan."

The flashlight beams were getting closer. One grazed the tree limb right over our heads. "Mooch, what's taking so long?"

"This isn't easy. I can't see a . . . here it is! I found the opening." Mooch grabbed Kevin's arm and pulled him down into the tunnel. I just hoped the noise we were making was being covered up by all the talking of the guys who were coming after us. I crawled into the tunnel behind Kevin and tried to give him a shove, but it threw him off balance, and he fell on his side.

"Don't push," he whispered. "I'm going as fast as I can." He started to pull himself along on his elbows, but it was taking forever. Suddenly a flashlight beam cut through the brush and landed on my arm. I froze.

"Look what I found," a low male voice said.

My heart was beating so loudly, I was sure I wasn't the only one who could hear it. I felt like a rabbit that had been spotted by a dog. I tried not to move a muscle, but my nose twitched.

Then the flashlight beam shifted to our campfire. "Told you I smelled smoke. Somebody just put out a fire." In the flashlight beams, I could see some guy squat by the fire site. He pulled his hand back sharply. "Ouch! Some of these embers are still hot. They can't be far from here." Shafts of light criss-crossed the clearing again. Another one caught me, but then moved on.

"Come on, you guys, this case of beer is getting heavy. Are you going to spend all night playing de-tective, or are we going to get back to the ore bed and party?"

The FBI had beer parties? This seemed strange.

"We could party right here. It's closer."

"No way," a female voice said. "The only thing that got me through work today was knowing I'd get a swim tonight."

The guy with the case of beer dumped it on the ground. "You can get your swim later, dollface. I'm not moving another step until I have a little rest."

The girl poked at the embers of the fire with a stick. "All right. Find some dead branches to throw on these hot coals. Maybe we can get the fire going again."

The others started tossing sticks on the fire, and

pretty soon it caught. I could see them in the orange glow of the flames—three couples. They were at least high-school seniors, or maybe a little older. One guy turned on his radio, and another tossed cans of beer to the others.

All of a sudden I felt someone next to me. "Mooch," I whispered, "stay in the tent! You want them to see us?"

"They can't. The fire's got them blinded. I thought I knew that voice. That one with the radio is a friend of my brother's. Stay away from him. He's mean, especially when he's been drinking."

"Thanks for the advice. I was just about to go out there and introduce myself."

"Really?"

"Geez, Mooch, I'm kidding. Where's Kevin?"

"Right here. What's going on?" Kevin had his head and shoulders out of the tent.

"Just a party," Mooch said.

"Wow!" Kevin whispered. "Look at that!"

One of the girls was starting to dance all by herself.

"All right, dollface!" the radioman said. He aimed his flashlight beam at her like a spotlight, and the others did the same. She untied a scarf from her ponytail and let her hair fall loose over her shoulders as she swayed back and forth to the music. Then she started unbuttoning her blouse.

"Do you believe this?" Mooch squealed in my ear. "If she strips naked, I'm going to pass out."

"If you do, you'll miss all the good stuff," Kevin said, grinning. "We'll tell you about it later."

We all held our breath as we watched her dance. She let the blouse slip over her shoulders, shimmied out of it, then undid the zipper of her jeans.

Mooch punched me in the arm. "Scout camp will never be the same again." As the girl wriggled out of her jeans, inch by inch, Mooch must have punched me in the arm a hundred times, but I was too numb to feel it.

"Look at that," Mooch said, "purple underwear!"

"That's not underwear. It's a bathing suit."

"Oh, rats," Mooch whispered. "Well, maybe she'll keep going."

Suddenly the song ended. Everybody hooted and whistled, including Mooch, until I clamped my hand over his mouth.

"Go, baby, go," the radioman yelled. "You still got some more to take off."

"You wish!" the girl said, tying her hair back with the scarf. She picked up her jeans and blouse and slung them over her shoulder. "Come on, you turkeys, I'm going for a swim."

"What about the fire?"

"It'll go out. There's nothing around it to burn."

They gathered up their stuff and headed off toward the ore beds. I looked over at Kevin in the flickering light from the dying fire. For the first time since the accident, he looked as if he wanted to go on living.

Chapter 9

I woke up with a mosquito buzzing around my ear. Sunlight was streaming in through the tent opening and it was already starting to get hot.

I poked at Mooch's sleeping bag. "Wake up, you guys. We have a big day ahead of us."

Mooch rolled over. "There's no school today, Ma. Let me sleep."

Kevin sat up and motioned for me to keep quiet. "Yes, there is school, son," he said in a high-pitched voice. "You get your big ugly body out of that bed and onto the school bus."

"Aw, Ma, can't I sleep a few more minutes?" Mooch blinked a few times, then opened his eyes. "That was a dirty trick, you guys. What time is it?"

I looked at my watch. "It's almost eight o'clock."

Kevin dug through the food bag and pulled out the dried backpacking food. "Dried-up beef stew. Is this all we have for breakfast?"

"No, that was just in case we got extra hungry last night. There're Cheerios and doughnuts for breakfast."

Kevin dumped the backpack out on the ground. All that came out were the packets of backpacking food.

"I know I packed the breakfast stuff," I said. "Did you see it, Mooch?"

"Who, me?" Mooch had that real innocent look on his face that meant he was guilty.

I pulled down the zipper of his sleeping bag. A half-eaten doughnut rolled out. "You ate our breakfast, didn't you?"

"I couldn't help it," Mooch whined. "I woke up in the middle of the night and I couldn't get back to sleep. I do that a lot at home."

"Now what are we going to do?" Kevin said. "I'm starved."

I picked up a package of beef stew. "This stuff isn't bad. All you do is add water and heat it up."

"We don't have any water," Mooch said. "You mixed it with the Kool-Aid."

"Besides, we don't have a pan," Kevin added.

"All right, all right! I'll sneak home and get some food," I said. "You two just sit tight until I get back. If you're outside and somebody comes, duck into the tent."

"Why should we hide?" Kevin asked. "Maybe

they'd have a way to get me out of here. I'm not going to be able to walk all the way back, you know."

I had to think of something fast. "But our camping trip's just started. We haven't had time to do anything yet. You'll feel better after you've had some breakfast."

Mooch climbed out of his sleeping bag. "Ryan is right, Kev. We're going to have to have a great time."

"And I'm going to get plenty of good stuff to eat, so just hang on, okay?" I didn't wait to hear the answer. I raced most of the way home, just slowing down long enough to catch my breath a few times. I couldn't tell if anybody was home as I ran into our backyard. I opened the back door slowly, so it wouldn't creak. There wasn't a sound in the house. Mom and Dad would be at work, but I didn't want to wake up Brenda.

I was just loading a package of hot dogs and a can of ravioli into my backpack when there was a knock at the door. I was going to ignore it, but there was more knocking—louder this time. I peeked out the back window. It was Mrs. Kowalski! I ran to open the door.

"Hi, Mrs. Kowalski. I was just . . . uh . . . starting breakfast."

She looked at the package in my hand. "Hot dogs?"

"Oh no, that's lunch. I like to plan ahead. That

way you can make sure you get all of the major food groups in by the end of the day." I was laying it on too thick. I always run off at the mouth when I'm nervous.

"Kevin won't be staying through lunch." Mrs. Kowalski smiled and came into the kitchen. "I thought I'd check up on him. Where is he?"

"Oh, he's still asleep."

"Oh dear, he didn't get overtired, did he?" She was edging toward the stairs. "Maybe I'd just better go up and see how he's doing."

"Uh . . . I wouldn't go up there, Mrs. Kowalski."

"Why not?"

"On account of Mooch."

"What about Mooch?"

What about Mooch? What? *What?* My mind was racing. "Because he . . . he sleeps in his underwear. It's not a pretty sight, believe me."

Mrs. Kowalski laughed. "For heaven's sake, Ryan, I've seen boy's underwear before."

"Not like this underwear," I said, hoping I wouldn't have to elaborate.

Just then Emily came bursting through the door. "Mom! I've been looking all over for you. There's a phone call for you."

"Find out who it is and tell them I'll call them back, Emily," Mrs. Kowalski said. "I want to go up and see Kevin."

"They said it was *very* important."

"Oh, all right." Mrs. Kowalski started out the door.

"So, Mrs. Kowalski, is it okay if Kevin stays for lunch? He's having a great time."

Mrs. Kowalski sighed. "Well . . . I guess it's all right, but make sure he gets home by one o'clock. I'm sure he'll need a nap today."

"Thanks, Mrs. Kowalski."

Emily hung back by the door as her mother walked down the driveway. "I'm sorry, Ryan. Mom got away when I wasn't looking. I have to watch her every second."

"Just make sure she doesn't slip away again. We'd be in real trouble if I hadn't come back this morning. That phone call came just in the nick of time, too."

"There wasn't any phone call," Emily said proudly. "I made it up when I saw her coming over here."

"Good thinking. Did you leave your phone off the hook?"

Emily looked puzzled. "No, why?"

"If she sees that the receiver's not off the hook, she'll know you were lying and she'll get suspicious. Come on, we have to get there before she does."

Mrs. Kowalski had gone the front way, so we ran

through the back fields. I slipped through the Kowalskis' kitchen door, grabbed the receiver off the
wall, and put it on the table. Suddenly I heard the
front door open. I couldn't get out the back door,
because Mrs. Kowalski had a clear view of it from
the front hall, so I shut myself into the utility closet.
The ironing board leaning on the closet wall started
to open, backing me into the spice shelf. One of
those spices was really strong. My nose started to
twitch.

"Hello? Is anybody there? Hello?" For a second,
I thought Mrs. Kowalski was talking to me, but then
she slammed down the phone. I heard Emily come
in the door.

"They hung up," Mrs. Kowalski said. "Do you
have any idea who it was?"

"Maybe it was just somebody selling something."

"I thought you said it was important."

"I don't know. It sounded important."

"Well, I'm going back to check on Kevin."

Now what was I going to do? Come on, Emily.
Think of something. The spice was burning my eyes
now. All of a sudden, I felt it coming. I sneezed.

"What was that?" Mrs. Kowalski asked.

"What?"

"I heard a sneeze."

"That's the cat," Emily said. "I think she has a

cold. Can we go to the store and get some English muffins for breakfast? There's nothing here but Dad's yucky bran cereal."

"All right, but I want to stop off and see Kevin on the way."

"Aw, Mom, leave him alone. You don't want to embarrass him in front of his friends again."

"When have I ever embarrassed Kevin in front of his friends?"

"Did you forget about McDonald's?"

There was a short pause, then I heard Mrs. Kowalski picking up her car keys. "Well, I guess he'll be all right for a few more hours."

"Sure, why wouldn't he be?" Emily said. "After all, he's only three houses away."

I listened as the car pulled out of the driveway before slipping out and going back home.

I stood in front of the refrigerator, trying to figure out what to take. "Let's see, if we have hot dogs, we'll need ketchup and mustard."

Just then, Brenda came in. "Who were you talking to?"

"Myself. I was just planning my day."

Brenda stuck her head in the refrigerator. "You're getting weirder by the minute." She pulled out a half-gallon of milk and drank some right from the container, then looked at me. "What are you doing with those hot dogs?"

"Just reading the list of ingredients. Did you ever stop to think what's in a hot dog?"

"Never. I don't read food, I eat it."

I sat down at the table and pretended to be reading the box of cereal. She came over and grabbed it away from me. "I hate to interrupt you in the middle of a chapter, but I want some breakfast."

She dumped cereal in a bowl, slopped some milk over it, and began eating. "I thought you were sleeping over at Mooch's house."

"I did, but there wasn't anything for breakfast."

"That doesn't surprise me. That's probably why he eats over here all the time." She looked up. "What are you staring at?"

"Nothing." Why didn't she hurry up? I'd already wasted too much time with Mrs. Kowalski. I sat there and counted from one to a hundred in my head. She still hadn't finished.

That's when I figured it out. Why was I in a hurry? My family didn't know I'd been in the woods overnight, Kevin's mother thought he was still asleep upstairs, and Mrs. Manuse wouldn't give Mooch a thought.

Brenda got up and dumped the last of her cereal and milk into the cat's dish. "I want to go to the movies with some of my friends this afternoon. You stay out of trouble, you hear? I'm responsible for you until Mom and Dad get home from work."

"I'll be over at Mooch's house. Besides, when have I ever been in trouble?" My voice squeaked on the word "trouble."

She looked at me funny for a minute, then shook her head and went upstairs. I took a quick inventory of my backpack and remembered to grab an old pan. Then I filled a gallon jug with water and took off. I couldn't believe how well everything was working out. If Emily could just keep track of her mother, we'd be safe until one o'clock. That gave me three and a half more hours to work on Kevin. It wasn't a lot, but I'd have to make the best of it.

Chapter 10

Mooch already had a fire going when I got back. "It's about time. What did you get? Bacon and eggs? Sausage?"

"Not exactly. Hot dogs and canned ravioli."

"For breakfast?"

"It's a combination breakfast and lunch. They call it brunch."

"Is that something you read about in one of your stupid books?"

Kevin crawled out of the tunnel. "Who cares what it is. It's food and I'm starved."

We cooked the hot dogs on sticks and I heated up the ravioli in the pan. I didn't bug Kevin about opening the can this time. At least he was trying. He even got his own hot dog on the stick without asking for help.

Mooch ate four hot dogs and most of the ravioli.

"Too bad you didn't like my choice of food," I said. "I guess it spoiled your appetite."

"Don't be smart, Ryan." Mooch was busy trying to eat the bits of ravioli that had burned on the bottom of the pan. "Things just taste better when you eat them outdoors."

"Okay," I said, checking my watch, "it's time for our next camping project. Kevin missed all the meetings where we learned knots."

"Oh yeah," Mooch said, "we're working on the merit badge for Emergency . . . what is it, Ryan?"

"Emergency Preparedness. We learned the knots you use for rescues."

"This ought to be easy for you, Kev," Mooch said, "you've always been a whiz at knots."

I got some rope out of my backpack. "I'll show you one. This is called the bowline, and you use it for pulling people out of ravines." I tied the knot slowly so he could see each step, then handed him a second piece of rope. "Here, you try it. You can do most of it with your right hand, so it shouldn't be a problem."

He twisted the rope around in his hand, then pulled an end through, but the knot fell out. "I can't, it's too hard."

"No, it isn't. I just showed you too fast. Here, we'll make the knot at the same time, step by step. Start with an overhand loop. That's good. Now,

bring the rope up through the loop and around the
standing part, then . . . wait, Kev. Go through the
loop first then around . . ."

Kevin threw the rope on the ground. "I told you.
I can't do this."

"Quit bugging him, Ryan," Mooch said.

"No, wait, I have another idea. I'm going to stand
behind you and put your hands through the mo-
tions. Here, grab the rope. Now here's the overhand loop, and we're going to bring the end up
through here . . . good." His left arm felt rigid, but
mostly it just had to hold the rope, so it didn't matter. ". . . and now we come back through the loop
and pull to tighten it. Great. You want to try it on
your own now?"

"Not yet. Show me one more time."

I ended up showing him four more times.

"Okay," Kevin said finally, "I think I have it. First
you make an overhand loop, then . . ." He stopped.

"Then what?" I prompted.

He bit his lip, trying to remember. "You bring
the rope through the . . ." He just stood there.

"Through the what, Kev? Think."

"I *am* thinking. I can't remember."

"Through the loop! Just look at it. It's right in
front of you. It couldn't be easier."

Kevin flung the rope across the campsite. "It may
be easy for you, but it's not for me. And I don't care

about any stupid merit badge." He headed for the tent.

I started to follow him, but Mooch stopped me. "Knock it off, Ryan. It's not going to work. Maybe he's not like he used to be. Maybe his mother was right all along."

"How is he ever going to know what he can do if he never tries?" I tried to push past Mooch, but he blocked me again.

"You're just making him feel worse."

"But he's got to keep trying."

Mooch grabbed me by the shoulders. "Wake up, will you? I told you this plan wasn't going to work. Kevin is as good as he's ever going to get. You gotta quit feeling sorry for . . ."

I gave Mooch a shove, knocking him to the ground. "I don't feel sorry for Kevin. That's the worst thing you can do to him. He'll never shape up if you pity him."

Mooch got to his feet and brushed himself off. "That's not what I was going to say. What I meant was, you gotta stop feeling sorry for *yourself*. You lost your best friend and you can't take it. You're the one who's gotta shape up." He went into the tent.

I thought about what Mooch had said. He was partly right. I had lost Kevin as a friend, at least the Kevin I knew. If only I could find something that

Kevin was still good at—something he could do better than Mooch or me.

He used to be able to swim better than anybody
else in our whole troop. There was an aboveground
pool in the Kowalskis' backyard. Kevin had learned
to swim when he was in first grade—really swim,
not just splash around wearing life preservers like
Mooch and me. Maybe he could still do it. Swimming was like riding a bicycle. Once you learned,
you'd never forget how, no matter what happened.

I called into the tent: "Come on out, you guys, I
have a great idea."

"We've had enough of your great ideas," Mooch
yelled back.

"No, really, you're going to like this one."

Mooch came out first. "I told Kevin I'd take him
home. We're going to walk a little at a time, and rest
in between. If he gets too tired, I'll carry him part-
way."

I could tell it wouldn't do any good to argue with
Mooch. That would only make him more stubborn.
"Okay, you can take him back. I'll even help you,
but let's do one thing just for fun before we leave."

Kevin had come up behind Mooch and was eye-
ing me with suspicion. "Like what?"

"Swimming. We could go back to the ore beds."

"Those ore beds are deep, Ryan," Mooch said.

"My brother told me some of them don't even have a bottom."

"How deep could they be? Ore beds are just the pits that were left after they mined out the strips of iron ore, and they didn't dig that deep. Besides lots of kids swim back there and nobody's ever drowned."

"Yeah, *big* kids," Mooch said. "I don't swim that good."

Kevin looked at Mooch. "It could be fun, and it's getting pretty hot. You wouldn't even have to swim. We could just go wading to cool off."

"Right," I said, putting my arm around Kevin's shoulders, and heading him toward the ore bed. "That cool water is going to feel great."

"Come back here, Ryan," Mooch said. "You're going to try something crazy."

Kevin laughed. "Old straight-arrow Ryan do something crazy? I don't think so."

Chapter 11

Mooch argued with me all the way to the ore bed, but I just kept going, and I kept Kevin going, too. He had to stop and rest a few times, but he liked the idea of going for a swim, and Mooch couldn't talk him out of it.

When we got there, we found some signs of the party the night before. "What slobs," I said. "Wouldn't you think they could clean up their lousy beer cans?"

Kevin was stooping down to pick something up.

"Never mind that now, Kev," I said. "We can clean it up before we leave."

"Look. Do you think it belonged to her?" Kevin held up a red silk scarf and had a goofy smile on his face.

"Yeah," Mooch said, "she had it in her hair, remember?"

Kevin sniffed the scarf and rolled his eyes. "Perfume. Like lilacs."

I grabbed it from him and knotted it loosely around his neck. "Here. Knights used to wear their fair lady's scarf into battle."

Kevin picked up a dead branch and waved it like a sword. "Charge!" he yelled, as he started toward the water.

I grabbed his arm. "Begging your pardon, Sir Kevin, but I think your swim would be more pleasant without the sneakers."

Kevin grinned. "Oh, yeah." He sat down and started pulling at his laces.

"Listen, you guys," Mooch said, "I don't think we ought to go swimming here."

I looked out over the ore bed as it sparkled in the sunlight. It was a long, thin pond, not more than a hundred yards wide. It curved around as it stretched off into the distance, so you couldn't see the other end of it. "Well, I don't know about Sir Kevin, here," I said, "but I can't wait to get in that cool water."

Kevin pulled off his second sneaker and got to his feet. "Me too. As I said before, charge!"

The two of us grabbed hands and splashed into the water, leaving Mooch behind on the shore. As our feet stirred up the ore-filled sandy bottom, the water turned rusty orange around us. It didn't look too great, but it felt wonderful.

"You gotta learn to swim one of these days, Mooch," I yelled over my shoulder. "You don't know what you're missing."

"I'll learn," Mooch said, "but not here."

Kevin pulled the back of the scarf up over his head like a kerchief. "Ooooh, I'd just love to go swimming," he said in a high-pitched voice, "but I'm afraid I'd get my pretty little feet wet." He disappeared under the water and sprang up again, laughing. This was the Kevin I remembered.

Mooch sat on the shore, hugging his knees, not saying anything.

"It's only up to my waist, Mooch," I shouted, but he just looked away.

Kevin grabbed my arm. "He'll get over it. Let's swim." At first, he looked a little awkward, but after a few strokes, you could hardly tell which was his bad arm. He stood up, still only waist deep. "This is great. We should do this every day."

"Sure, I'll swim with you anytime you want." I followed him as he swam back along the shore. Then he veered out and headed toward the middle.

"Don't go out too far," I yelled, "there might be a drop-off."

Kevin suddenly turned with a panicked expression on his face. He disappeared under the surface, then came back up. "Help! I'm drowning!"

"Hang on, I'm coming." I swam as fast as I could to get to him. I saw his head slip under water again, and he came up sputtering and thrashing just as I got to him.

"Calm down," I shouted, "I'll pull you in!"

He went under again and came up with the knot from the scarf on top of his head like a bow. "My hero!" he said in a high voice, folding his hands under his chin.

"You're . . . you're standing up. You weren't in trouble at all."

"Sorry," he said, fluttering his eyelashes, "my mistake."

"That wasn't funny, Kevin," Mooch yelled. "I thought you were really drowning."

I got out of the water and sat down next to Mooch, trying to catch my breath.

"Aw, come on, you two," Kevin yelled, "what happened to your sense of humor?"

"Mine just drowned," I shouted back, coughing.

We watched Kevin swimming back and forth. He moved with smooth, even strokes, barely rippling the surface of the water.

Mooch was busy fussing with a piece of rope.

"What are you doing?"

"I'm tying a bowline, just in case I have to haul one of you idiots out of the water."

"Don't worry, Mooch, nobody's going to drown. Look at him out there. You'd never know he'd been in an accident."

"You're pushing him too far, Ryan."

"Who's pushing? Am I forcing him to swim right now?"

Mooch squinted at the water. "He's going out toward the middle."

"Relax, will you?"

Kevin's head went under the water. Then he came up and started yelling for help.

"Quit fooling around, Kevin," Mooch yelled.

"Let him have some fun. It seems good to see him acting goofy again."

We watched him thrash around in the water, ducking under and bobbing up again. He was doing a good imitation of a drowning man. Even Mooch finally had to laugh at him. Then I noticed something that made me stop laughing. Kevin was only using his right hand, and the left one was curled up into a tight fist.

"He's not kidding this time," I said, running for the water. "He's in trouble. Get help."

"Where?" Mooch was right. We were too far away from help. I had to save Kevin myself.

He was farther out than I thought. He went under again, but he surfaced just before I got to him. His eyes were wild, and he grabbed me with his good hand. He had me around the neck, and his weight pushed me under. I squirmed out of his grip and broke through to the surface.

"Ryan, grab the rope!" Mooch tossed the line. It snaked through the air and landed about ten feet away.

"I can't reach. Throw it again," I shouted, just before Kevin got me in another hammerlock and we went under again. When we came back up, I saw Mooch wading out into the water, gathering up the rope.

"Don't grab me, Kev," I said, trying to get a grip on him, "just let me hold you up. Mooch is going to throw us a line."

Kevin seemed to calm down a little, but he still clung to me. Mooch threw the line, but it fell short again. He hauled it in and came farther out into the water. Suddenly, he disappeared. "Mooch must have dropped off a ledge," I yelled. "He'll drown if we don't get to him."

Kevin didn't seem to hear me. He tried to climb on my shoulders, pushing me under. I pried his fingers off my arm, and when we reached the surface, I was free of him. Mooch was thrashing around in the water yelling for help. I couldn't save them both. They were too far apart, and they were both panicked. Besides, I was so exhausted from wrestling with Kevin, I could barely tread water to keep myself afloat.

Then an amazing thing happened. Kevin looked over and saw Mooch. "Hang on, Mooch," he yelled, "I'm coming!"

I couldn't believe it. He started swimming toward Mooch, pulling with just his right arm. His face was twisted up in pain, but he kept going. I was so tired, I could barely move, but I headed after him.

When Kevin reached Mooch, he gave him a hard shove toward shore with his good hand. Mooch went under for a second, but then stumbled to his feet in chest-deep water. I came up behind them and we all hung onto each other as we dragged ourselves back onto the shore and collapsed in a heap. Nobody said anything. All we could do was cough and gag.

Chapter 12

"You guys okay?" I asked when I could catch my breath.

"Yeah," Mooch gasped, rolling over on his back. "No thanks to you. That was a dumb idea. This whole thing was a dumb idea. I've been telling you that all along."

"I know, I *know!*" I looked over at Kevin. He was just lying there, staring up at the sky. "How about you, Kev, you feel all right?"

Kevin still didn't say anything.

"Geez, now look what you did," Mooch said, "he can't even talk."

I edged closer to Kevin. "Hey, buddy, how you doing? Kev?"

Mooch scrambled to his feet and came around behind me. "You think he's dead?"

"Don't be stupid. He's breathing, isn't he? You ever see a dead person breathe?"

"I never saw a dead person do anything," Mooch whispered.

Suddenly Kevin mumbled something.

I leaned in closer. "What did you say, Kev?"

Kevin sat up and shook his head. "I swam. Can you believe it? I was really swimming."

"You were swimming, all right," Mooch said, sitting down next to him. "You saved my life."

"I know. I didn't even think about whether I could do it or not. I just knew I had to get to you."

Mooch punched him in the arm. "Yeah, you really did it, buddy. If it weren't for you, I'd probably be at the bottom of that ore bed right now."

Kevin shook his head again and looked out over the ore bed. "This was a wild idea—kidnapping me and all."

"Yeah," Mooch said, "but it's going to get even wilder if we don't get back home."

For once, Mooch was right about something. I looked at my watch. It was noon. "Okay, we only have an hour to get Kevin home. Mooch, run and get the four-wheeler to pick Kevin up."

Kevin stood up. "What's the matter with me walking?"

"I don't think you should, Kev," I said. "It's a long ways out of here."

"I know how far it is, but I think I could make it if we go slow and stop a lot."

Mooch looked at me and shrugged. "If he wants to do it, let's go for it." I could tell Mooch wasn't wild about the idea of running all the way home.

We put our sneakers on and started back toward the campsite. Kevin seemed tired, but he was doing all right. We walked along in silence for a while, then Kevin stopped. "Maybe I could go to camp after all, you know? If I can swim, I could do the waterfront stuff."

Mooch grinned. "Oh, sure, you could hang around all day with the gorgeous waterfront counselor. You're no dummy, Kowalski."

"No, really. I'm going to tell Mom that I have to go to camp. I know Dad will back me up. I can do a lot more than they think I can. I wouldn't have known that if we hadn't come out here."

I tried to give Mooch my "I told you so" look, but he ignored me.

It didn't take long to get back to the campsite. We went into the tent and stretched out on our sleeping bags to rest.

"Too bad we used up all of our food," I said. "I sure could use a snack about now, and I don't mean dried beef stew."

Mooch burrowed into the bottom of his sleeping bag and came up with a whole bag of Milky Ways.

"How come you didn't tell us you had those?" Kevin asked.

Mooch offered the bag to Kevin. "I was saving them for an emergency."

"Great," Kevin said, helping himself, "this definitely qualifies as an emergency."

After we rested and munched for a while, I started to feel better. Kevin must have, too, because he talked nonstop about camp and all the neat stuff we could smuggle in to sell to the other kids. If he had his way, we'd be millionaires by the end of two weeks.

"We'd better get started," I said finally. "I want to get back before they start looking for us."

Mooch held his stomach. "I wouldn't mind being found about now. I don't feel so good."

"You must have eaten at least a dozen candy bars," I said. "The exercise will be good for you."

Kevin put on his helmet and we began walking through the woods with me in the lead and Mooch bringing up the rear. We hadn't gone too far when Kevin had to sit down on a log. "Maybe that idea about Mooch getting the four-wheeler wasn't too bad. I don't think I can make it all the way back. Not after everything that's happened."

Mooch patted him on the shoulder. "Don't worry about it, Kev. You wait here and I'll go get it. That's the least I can do after you saved my life." Mooch started out, then came back. "Hey, what day is it today?"

"Thursday," I said.

"Uh-oh, it's Gary's day off. If he's home, I won't be able to sneak off with the four-wheeler."

"Couldn't you just ask him to help us?" I asked.

"Yeah, maybe I could. Gary's cool. He wouldn't tell anybody." Mooch headed off through the woods.

"It doesn't matter if Gary tells now, anyway," Kevin said. "If I want to go to camp, I'll have to tell Mom about camping out here."

All of a sudden, telling Mrs. Kowalski about our overnight in the woods didn't sound like such a great idea. I sat down on the log next to Kevin. "Let's play it by ear when we get back, Kev. I'm not sure you should mention anything about saving Mooch. Your mother might really get bent out of shape about us swimming in the ore bed."

"You're right. That was a pretty dangerous thing to do."

"Besides, what's important is that *you* know you saved Mooch's life."

"Yeah, I guess." Kevin was quiet for a minute. "Sorry I pooped out on you like this. It would have been better if I could have walked out of here."

"That's okay. I'm not so sure I could have made it back myself." I fished the rope from my pocket and tied a couple of knots in it.

Kevin reached for the rope. "Let me see that thing for a minute." He made a few tries tying the bowline, then gave up. He dropped the rope and put his head in his hands. "I feel so dumb when that happens, like I've been invaded by an alien and it's controlling my brain. Sometimes I think it would have been easier if I'd been killed."

I pictured Kevin lying in the ditch. "That day . . . the day you got hit . . . I didn't help you. I just stood there."

Kevin looked up. "You never told me that."

"I never told anybody."

"So why are you bringing it up now?"

"I don't know. It just bothers me. I keep thinking I should have done something, that's all."

Kevin shrugged. "What were you going to do? You're no doctor. Besides, they say people got there right away to help. You would've done something if we'd been all alone."

I closed my eyes. I could almost feel the people jostling me, shoving past me to get to Kevin—the man who was driving the car, a truck driver, and then the ambulance medics. And all through it, I couldn't move a muscle. I could feel my eyes filling with tears.

"It wasn't your fault that I got hit, Ryan. You know that, don't you?"

"Yeah, I guess," I said, but the words caught in my throat. I wiped my eyes with the sleeve of my T-shirt.

"If it bothers you to be around me," Kevin said quietly, "it's okay."

"It's not that. It's just that I was so scared to see what you'd be like after the accident."

"You were scared! How do you think I felt? I figured you guys wouldn't want to have anything to do with me. I'm not the same as I was before, and I never will be. They told me that at the rehab center."

"What do you mean?" I asked. "You're getting better already. You hardly walk with a limp anymore, and you've even been using your left hand a little bit today."

Kevin took a deep breath. "My arm and leg are going to be okay. That's not what I meant. I'm just . . . different."

"Different? How?"

"It's my brain. It just doesn't always work the way I want it to. Like when I try to make a phone call or tie a knot. I can't always get everything in the right order."

I couldn't think of anything to say.

"Look," Kevin said, after a long minute of silence had passed, "I'll understand if you don't want to be friends anymore."

"Why wouldn't I want to be friends? Because you can't call me up or tie a stupid knot?"

"No, because I'm not the person you knew, and I may act goofy sometimes."

"I hate to break this to you," I said, putting my arm around Kevin's shoulder, "but you've been acting goofy ever since kindergarten."

Kevin picked up a stick and began breaking pieces off from it. "What does Mooch think about all this?"

"That's a stupid question. You know Mooch doesn't think. Besides, you saved his life. In some cultures that would make him your slave forever."

"I sure could use a slave, but a friend would be better."

"Don't worry, you've got two of them. Hey, listen, somebody's coming." I could hear the motor of the four-wheeler. Pretty soon it came into sight with Gary driving. Mooch wasn't with him.

"You guys are in big trouble," Gary said, as he pulled to a stop. "Everybody's been looking for you for the past couple of hours. They were ready to call the police when Mooch showed up. Kevin's mother really lit into him, and he took off for home."

"Why were they looking for us?" I asked. "We weren't supposed to be back until one."

Gary handed me the helmet. "Check your watch, Ryan, it's past three."

Both hands on my watch were still pointing to

twelve. It must have stopped when we were in the ore bed. "I guess this isn't waterproof anymore," I said.

"Is my mother really mad?" Kevin asked.

"Hysterical is more like it." Gary climbed on the four-wheeler and motioned for us to get on behind. "She called your father at work and had him come home."

We didn't say anything else on the way back. When you're about to get killed, you don't exactly feel like discussing it. I tried to think up a good story. Nobody was going to believe the real reason I'd come up with the kidnapping plan. It didn't even make sense to *me* anymore. Mom and Dad might understand, but try explaining to Mrs. Kowalski. She'd probably have me arrested.

As we came through the opening in the Lockwoods' hedgerow, I could see Kevin's whole family waiting for us in their backyard. Mrs. Kowalski made a dive for Kevin as soon as Gary pulled up by the aboveground swimming pool. "My poor baby, what have they done to you?" She lifted him off the four-wheeler and rocked him back and forth in her arms. "And you!" she screamed at me. "What on earth did you think you were doing, dragging Kevin into the woods like that? You and Malcolm are never to come near Kevin again, do you hear?"

Emily stepped forward. "Ryan and Mooch aren't

the only ones to blame. I knew what they were going to do all along."

Mrs. Kowalski turned on her. "What? You knew and you didn't tell me?"

"Nobody can tell you anything, Mom," Emily said. "You never listen to us. Ryan was just trying to help Kevin get better."

Mr. Kowalski put his arm around Emily. "Let's try to calm down and find out what's happened here, Greta. Give Ryan a chance to explain himself."

All of a sudden, everyone was looking at me. This was worse than giving an oral book report at school. Much worse. "I thought if we got Kevin away from . . . well, off in the woods," I began, "he could try some camping stuff. I just wanted to show him he could do more than he thought he could."

"I'm so sick of hearing about this camping nonsense," Mrs. Kowalski said. "I'm only going to say this one more time. Kevin is *not* going to camp."

"But, Mrs. Kowalski, I just thought . . ."

"No, you didn't think, Ryan. You just rushed headlong into a foolish, dangerous plan."

"Wait a minute!" Kevin's voice was so loud, it shocked everyone into silence. He pushed away from his mother and stood facing her. "I know better than any of you what I can and can't do. Ryan showed me that back in the woods. I'm not a baby,

Mom, and you've got to stop treating me like one. I'll be fine at camp. And if there's some stuff I can't do, it won't matter. I just want to be there with my friends."

"Kevin's right, Greta," Mr. Kowalski said quietly, "we need to give him some room now. Let him recover at his own pace."

Mrs. Kowalski started to cry. "Kevin, I only want what's best for you. I just couldn't stand it if you got hurt again."

"I know, Mom, but you can't go around for the rest of my life protecting me. I'm going to be okay. Watch. I'll show you something." He walked over to the pool, took off his helmet, and started up the ladder.

Mrs. Kowalski started after him. "Kevin, be careful. You shouldn't be climbing."

Mr. Kowalski stopped her and held her gently by the shoulders as Kevin walked across the deck and started climbing down into the pool. "Look, Greta," Mr. Kowalski said, "he's using his left hand on the ladder."

"Here goes," Kevin shouted. He ducked in to get his shoulders wet, then swam across the pool with smooth, even strokes. He stood up at the other side. "How was that?"

"I don't believe it," Mrs. Kowalski said, gripping the rim of the pool. "That's wonderful, Kevin. You

should swim every day now. It would be good therapy for you."

Kevin swam over to her. "Camp would be good
therapy, too, Mom. Are you going to let me go?"

Mrs. Kowalski reached over and brushed the wet
hair out of Kevin's eyes. "It's too soon to say, Kevin.
Maybe if you could prove to me in the next few
weeks that you're ready. . . . I just don't think you
are."

After all we had gone through, she still wasn't
planning to let him go. I could barely look at Kevin
when I said good-bye.

I had to explain everything to Mom and Dad
when they got home from work, but I still left out
the part about the ore bed. I knew we'd never take
a chance on swimming back there again.

Mom was madder than I've ever seen her. "I'm so
disappointed in you, Ryan. You've never lied to me
before." She banged her hand on the kitchen table
when she said the word "lied."

"But, Mom, would you have let me take Kevin
back into the woods if you'd known about it?"

"No, of course not, but we could have helped him
gradually. It didn't have to be accomplished in one
day."

"It's just that camp is coming up so soon. We
didn't have time to mess around. He really wants to
go, Mom."

Mom's face softened. "I know how you feel, Ryan. You did the wrong thing, but you did it for the right reasons. Kevin is lucky to have you as a friend."

"Yeah, a lot of good I did."

Dad came over and messed up my hair. "You may not have proved anything to Mrs. Kowalski, son, but it sounds as if you proved something to Kevin. Wait and see what happens between now and camp."

I rode my bike past Kevin's house the next morning and saw him sitting in the backyard, working on something. I couldn't see Mrs. Kowalski anywhere, so I rode into the yard.

"Nice helmet," he said, when he saw me. "You trying to look like me?"

I undid the chin strap of the bike helmet and took it off. "Mom made me get it after the accident. She said if we'd been wearing helmets that day you might not have been hurt as bad."

Kevin was sanding away at a baseball bat. "Yeah, I've heard that about a million times. The helmet's not bad, though. It makes you look like one of those racers in the Tour de France."

I put down my bike and sat next to him on the grass. "Yeah, that's me—world class racer. What happened to the bat?"

"I just found it under a bush. It must have been

outside ever since the accident. I think it'll be okay
after I get it smoothed out. I can't find the ball,
though."

"I'll bring mine over. We can try a little batting
practice later if you want."

Kevin grinned. "Sure. Just don't expect any home
runs from me."

"Since when did you ever hit any home runs?"

Kevin put down the bat. "You know what my dad
told me? He already signed me up for camp, to
make sure I could get in the same session with you
and Mooch. He's not telling Mom, though."

"That's great! You're definitely going?"

Kevin shook his head. "No, I still have to prove to
Mom that I'm ready."

"These next few weeks are your big chance, Kev.
You have to really work to show your mom you're
going to be okay."

"I know. I'm going to stop worrying about what I
can't do, and concentrate on the things I can do.
Dad and Emily are on my side, so that should help."

"Speaking of Emily, you could win a few points
with her by doing the dishes once in a while."

Kevin made a face. "Dishes? Are you kidding?
I'm not *that* desperate to go to camp."

"Sure you are. Besides, doing dishes isn't so bad.
Just think of it as swimming from the wrists down."

Kevin grinned again and poked me in the stomach with his bat. "Some friend you are!" Then his face got serious. He ran his hand back and forth over the smooth place on the bat for a minute, then looked up at me. "You really are, you know—some friend."